John Arthur Fraser

The Merry Cobbler

An Original Comedy Drama in Four Acts

John Arthur Fraser

The Merry Cobbler
An Original Comedy Drama in Four Acts

ISBN/EAN: 9783337054977

Printed in Europe, USA, Canada, Australia, Japan

Cover: Foto ©Andreas Hilbeck / pixelio.de

More available books at **www.hansebooks.com**

THE MERRY COBBLER

AN ORIGINAL COMEDY DRAMA

IN FOUR ACTS

BY

J. A. FRASER, JR.,

Author of A Noble Outcast—The Train Wreckers—Edelweiss
—McGinty's Troubles—Linked by Law—The Judge's
Wife—Under an Alias—Modern Ananias—The
New State's Attorney—Face to Face—
A Delicate Question—'Twixt
Love and Money—Etc.

CHICAGO:
THE DRAMATIC PUBLISHING COMPANY.

Cast of Characters.

Franz von Altenheim—A light-hearted cobbler.
Morris Holmes—An adventurer.
Col. Derrom—A leading lawyer.
I. L. Findham—A detective.
Levee Bob—A bad negro.
Mike Maloney—A police officer.
Stella Derrom—The Colonel's daughter.
Mrs. Rafferty—A " poor, lone widdy woman."
Mrs. Holmes—An ill-used wife and mother.
Rosalie—The banana girl.
Carlotta—Stella's bosom friend.
Leila
Flossie } Little friends of the merry cobbler.

NOTE. Mrs. Rafferty and Gretchen, **Findham and Col. Derrom**, Bob and Maloney may be easily doubled.

Plays one hour, forty-five minutes.

Author's Edition.

Printed from the original prompt book with all the stage business and relative positions of the characters, complete list of properties required, description of costumes etc. etc.

Copyrighted by J. A. Fraser, Jr. A. D. 1891.
Copyrighted by The Dramatic publishing Co., A. D. 1895.

Notice.

12-32382

Synoposis.

Act I. The Cobbler Baron — Plotting for a fortune — Franz's birthday party—Stella meets her fate—The runaway horse—Franz rescues Stella.

Act II. The plotter at work—Franz as a healthy invalid—The babies and their bouquet—Franz's courtship—The Colonel's wrath—Holmes' discomfiture.

Act III. Carlotta's party—Findham's fine work—Holmes anticipates triumph—Confronted by a wronged woman—Franz's stratagem—The kidnappers—"Dot's de kind of a sauerkraut I am."

Act IV. A big haul attempted—Ready for flight—Franz and Stella hear secrets—Gretchen, the accuser—A villain unmasked—The Baron von Altemheim—Restored to a brother's arms—Wedding bells.

Author's Notes on "The Merry Cobbler".

Had this piece been written with a special regard for the requirements of amateur players, it could not have been happier in its results. Rendered popular by Mr. John R. Cumpson, who has starred in the part of Franz with great success for several seasons, the play has gained a strong hold upon theatre goers by the simplicity of its story and the strong undercurrent of heart interest mingled with comedy low and high, light and broad. There is not a poor part in the piece. Even the policeman who has only a few lines to speak is sure of two or three good laughs, while Franz, Findham, Bob and Mrs. Rafferty are very "fat" in comedy. Stella is an ingenue part with excellent opportunities, and Gretchen, though short, is certain to make a hit. The children's parts are easy, and from six to ten youngsters may be effectively introduced, with their little Kindergarten songs, in Act II. They will be found effective, indeed, in every act of the play. Holmes is a villain who is not overdrawn and is defiant to the last. None of the parts are difficult, while the stage business, which is fully described, and the climaxes are simple to handle and very effective. The part of Franz, with a good makeup and a fair dialect, will be found to "play itself." If Franz can sing, so much the better and Rosalie has an opportunity to introduce a dance. The scenic effects are of the simplest description.

Costumes.

Franz. -Act I. Knee breeches, bluish grey stockings, ankle shoes, frock coat of quaint cut, either dark green or blue with metal buttons, red or fancy vest, red handkerchief around neck, neglige shirt, odd looking Dutch cap with big crown, shoemaker's apron and blond curly wig. He must look about 18 or 20 years—clean shaven. This costume must look old and shabby. Act II. Same breeches, shoes and stockings an old, faded dressing gown or smoking jacket. His right arm is in a sling. Act III. Black stockings and ankle shoes, black knee breeches, velveteen sack coat and vest, Stanley cap. For the change he has a high Normandy nurse's cap, blond wig with long plaits to hang down the back, a short knee skirt of dark material which slips over his breeches, the shoes and stockings being unchanged; white chemise waist very full sleeves and black Swiss boddice. The change must be quickly made, so skirt, boddice, etc., should be made to go on in one piece with as few hooks or tapes as possible. Act IV. Regulation evening dress. **Morris Holmes.**—Act I. Elegant morning dress, dark Prince Albert and light trousers, patent leather shoes, gloves. He should look about forty, slightly grey on the temples. Act II. The same costume may be worn or changed to tweed suit made if desired. Act. III. Regulation evening dress, silk hat and light over- coat. Act IV. Evening dress, silk hat, overcoat carried on arm. **Col. Derrom.**--Act. I. Business suit, slouch hat, black or grey and white hair, mustache and imperial, carries cane and wears gloves. To look about sixty and well preserved. No change is required in Act II unless the actor chooses. Acts III and IV. Evening dress. **Findham.**—Sporty looking suit of loud check tweed, white or grey, plug hat with black band, red face, bald wig, dissipated appearance. To look about thirty, but prematurely bald. Costume is not changed. **Bob.**—Act. I. Old jeans pants, pink striped calico shirt, "cowfeed" straw hat, much torn, brogans, crop nigger wig. Act II. Slightly better dressed, soft felt hat. Act III. Overalls, blue checked jumper and red cap with visor. **Mike Maloney.**—Regulation police uniform, red galway whiskers, red face. Made up very fat. **Stella.**--Should wear handsome walking costume in Acts I and II. In Act III. A pretty afternoon dress and in Act IV. Handsome full dress. **Mrs. Rafferty.**—Made up as an Irish woman of fifty years, fat with smooth red wig slicked down over forehead. She wears an apron ı latter acts. **Gretchen.**—Act III. Very poorly clad with black shawl over her head. Blond wig with long plaits similar to wig worn by Franz in this act. Act IV. Neat but plain dark street dress. No hat or bonnet. To look about twenty years. **Rosalie.** Act I. Knee skirts and jaunty hat. Same in Act II. Act III. Longer skirt, anything natty and pretty will do if it is not elaborate. A nice white pique or muslin with gray colored ribbon and simple straw hat will do nicely. Act IV. Ankle skirt quite in style, no hat. Rosalie should wear her hair down her back all through. To look about sixteen. **Carlotta.** Similiar to Stella's costumes. **Leila and Flossie.**—Pinafores and little close white caps for Acts I. and II. Act III. A little more elaborate and Act IV. A little more so.

Property List.

Act I. Cobbler's bench—rough pine bench for shoes to stand on—a packing case will do—a lot of old shoes, some new ones and one horse shoe—table for fruit stand with fruit and nuts on it—chair for Franz and chair for Rosalie—big rag doll wrapped in paper for the children—letter for Holmes—shoe with heel off for Stella and another with heel on for Franz to pretend mending—three nickels for Franz, boxes to set out the party—quarter for Holmes to throw—hammer, last and nails for Franz—pocket book with money in it for Stella—hand mirror for Franz at stall—flat slab of stone and two half cocoanut shells to produce noise of galloping horses—wood and metal crash for sound of collision.

Act II. Small table, large table, old arm chair and two other chairs, old sofa—old cracked vase—two or three plates and wine glasses on small table up c —cards, notebook and pencil for Findham—small stool for Stella to sit on—white handled razor for Bob—bouquet for children—paper money for Holmes—ring for Stella—small basket with bottle of wine, fruit, etc., for Stella.

Act III. Garden bench—two flasks for Findham—roll of paper money for Holmes—dagger for Gretchen—sheet of paper, folded, for Findham—revolver for Franz—steam boat whistle, gong to ring when boat stops, two sheet iron plates and wire brush to beat them to imitate noise of steam yacht.

Act IV. Portiers for c. door, table with table cover, carpet, arm chair, other chairs, sofa, rugs and other handsome furniture for an elegant set—legal documents for Colonel—newspaper and writing material on table—check book for Colonel—legal document for Gretchen—handcuffs for Holmes.

THE MERRY COBBLER
SCENE PLOTS

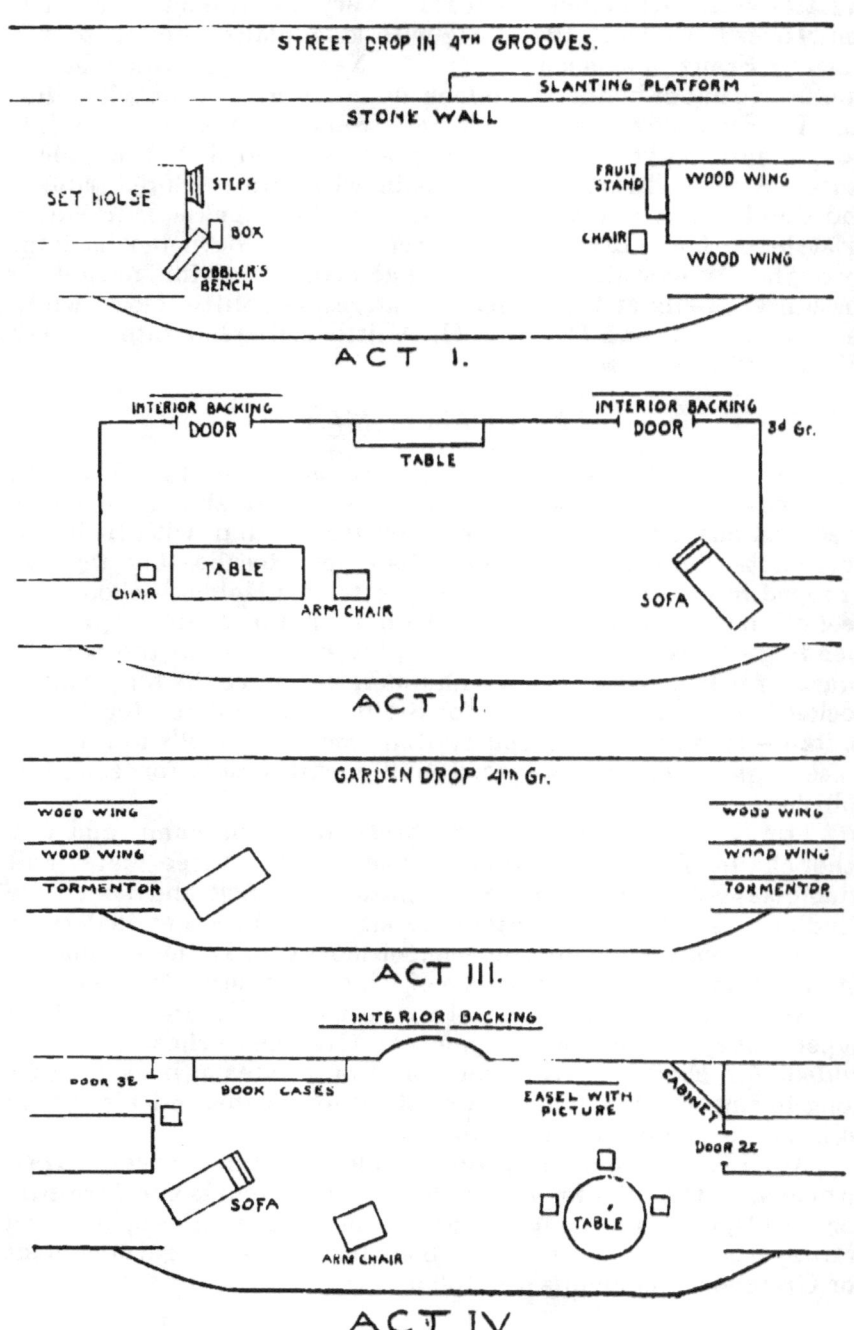

STREET DROP IN 4TH GROOVES.

SLANTING PLATFORM

STONE WALL

SET HOUSE STEPS BOX COBBLER'S BENCH

FRUIT STAND WOOD WING CHAIR WOOD WING

ACT I.

INTERIOR BACKING DOOR TABLE INTERIOR BACKING DOOR 3d Gr.

CHAIR TABLE ARM CHAIR SOFA

ACT II.

GARDEN DROP 4th Gr.

WOOD WING WOOD WING
WOOD WING WOOD WING
TORMENTOR TORMENTOR

ACT III.

INTERIOR BACKING

DOOR 3E BOOK CASES EASEL WITH PICTURE CABINET DOOR 2E

SOFA ARM CHAIR TABLE

ACT IV

THE MERRY COBBLER.

ACT I.

[*Set house* R. *with steps. Cobbler's bench below steps. Old and new shoes on rough bench beside it. Fruit stand* L. *with apples, oranges, bananas, nuts, etc. A stone wall about 5 feet high clear across at back with platform behind it slanting up from stage for children and Franz to climb over. Street backing. Chair at fruit stand and another inside door of house. Lively music at rise of curtain. Rosalie disc. tending fruit stand* L. *Bob enters* R. I. E. *whistling. Stops at fruit stand and handles fruit.*]

Bob. [*Holding up fruit.*] How much?

Ros. Three for a dime. [*Without rising and with evident contempt.*]

Bob. [*Holding up orange.*] How much?

Ros. Two bits a dozen.

Bob. Um, ah! [*Feels in pockets.*] Recken I won't neither. [*Laughs, puts hands in pockets and exits* R. U. E. *whistling.*]

Ros. [*Jumping up.*] Sassy nigger. [*Looking after* **Bob.**] He wouldn't have dared to do that if Franz had been here. I wonder where he is? I haven't seen him this morning. [*Buss. of dusting and arranging fruit.*]

Holmes. [*Enters* R. U. E. *with* Bob, *turns at entrance.*] See that you remain within call, for if you're not on hand when I want you I'll break every bone in your black hide.

Bob. Yes sah, I'll sho'ly be heah, sah.

Holmes. You'd better. [*Exit* Bob, Holmes *comes down. Aside.*] Deuced pretty girl. [*Aloud.*] Good morning, my dear.

Ros. I'm *not* your dear. I wouldn't be your dear for a hundred dollars. I know *you* Mr. Holmes and nothing whatever to your credit. Bzip! [*Making a dart at him.*] Don't touch me,

7

I'm dangerous. [*Exit into store.*]

Holmes. The little spit-fire. Ah, well—she's an exception to the general rule, that's all. [*Strolls leisurely down.*]

Derrom. [*Enters* R. 1. E.] Good morning, Morris, good morning.

Holmes. Good morning, Colonel, howdy? [*Shaking hands.*] Just on my way to your office.

Derrom. What can I do for you?

Holmes. I want your advice in a rather peculiar case. [*Down* L. C.]

Derrom. Nothing I delight in so much as peculiar cases. What is it?

Holmes. Well, as I told you when I first met you and your charming family, I am a widower, While traveling in Germany some years ago I fell madly in love with a girl, Gretchen Altenheim, who was the favorite niece of an old bachelor uncle and kept house for him. She eloped with me and we were married at Antwerp, immediately afterward taking passage to America.

Derrom. Quite romantic—well, what next?

Holmes. Our happiness, alas, was short lived, for in giving birth to a little daughter my poor Gretchen died and the baby only survived her a few hours.

Derrom. Poor fellow. [*Crosses* L.] Fate was indeed a cruel jade in you case. But why do you tell me all this?

Holmes. Because of this letter. [*Hands letter.*] Which I received by this morning's mail. It is from some German functionary and tells me that my late wife's uncle has died leaving a large fortune accumulated in his old age from the invention of a smokeless powder which was adopted by the Government.

Derrom. I see, I see, and he has remembered your wife in his will.

Holmes. On the contrary, he left no will at all and my wife, or her children, and her brother are the only heirs, so my correspondent informs me.

Derrom. And as she and her child are both dead, you fall heir to her share. Allow me to congratulate you. [L. C. *He is about to shake hands when* **Holmes** *stops him.*]

Holmes. [C.] More than that. This brother ran away from home on account of the old uncle's cruelty and miserly habits, and unfortunately fell a victim to yellow fever before he had been in this country three months.

Derrom. [*Shakes hands.*] Then you are the sole heir. I don't see anything peculiar in *this* case. It is as plain as daylight. [*Aside crossing* R.] What a match he will be for my Stella. -

Holmes. Not quite so plain as you think, my dear Colonel. The church in which our marriage was solemnized was burned shortly afterward and all the records were destroyed.

Derrom. But you have your wife's wedding certificate?

Holmes. No, that's just where the trouble is. Never dreaming of anything like this, I took no care to preserve it and haven't the slightest idea of where it is.

Derrom. Ah, this is serious. In order to establish your rights you will be compelled to make sufficient proofs of the deaths of the other three parties and also establish the fact that you were the legal husband of the old man's niece. You'd better come up to the house and have dinner with me tonight when we can talk this matter over at our ease. The girls will be glad to see you.

Holmes. Thanks—I shall avail myself of your kind invitation. I hope the young ladies are quite well——?

Derrom. Especially Stella—eh, you sly rascal. [*Nudges* **Holmes** *and chuckles.*] Well I must be off. [*Shakes hands.*] We shall expect you. Now, if you value my good opinion—and Stella's don't keep us waiting. [*Exit* L. I. E.]

Holmes. [*Calling after* **Derrom.**] I'll be prompt. [*Walking back and forth as if in thought.*] The first step is taken. Now for a desperate play which if successful will make me rich. The situation is in my own hands if my nerve does not fail me. Gretchen has not been heard of for four years and proofs of her death will be easily trumped up. The people who take care of the child have not the least idea of her true name so there is little or no danger from that quarter. The only difficulty lies in the proof of my marriage. Well, I'll get that if I have to write a certificate myself. [*As he turns to go* R. U. E. *children are heard singing back of wall.*] Hello, what is this?

Franz. [*Appears on wall, singing and assists children up to top of wall one after the other. All sing until chorus is finished.*] Vell, vell, vell. [*All laugh.*]

Holmes. [*Aside.*] My child.

Franz. [*Gets over wall.*] Now den—vone at a time bickause of you all yump togedder you make me some droubbles mit mein back alretty once. Now den Flossie. [*She jumps and he catches her, kisses her and tosses her in the air, catches her and sets her down.*] Vell, vell, vell. [*Laughs.*] Now den Tottie, you vas next ash der barber sait ven he got married de second time. [*Same buss.*] Ollie. [*Same buss.*] Ah—ven you get ten years older you von't yump into Franz's arm so kvick. [*Pause.*]- you'll be so heavy den he von't let you. [*Laugh.*] Aen, Leila—you vhas still

here like Humpity Dumpity oop on de vall—vell, vell, voll.
[*Laughs.*]   Yump.

Leila.   I'm afraid.

Franz.   Afrait mit your Lieber Franz?   Ach Himmel!   Look
oud—[*Pointing.*]—der Bogey man comes in front of you pack
wards.   [**Leila** *gives a little scream, half laughing and jumps.
Same buss.*]   Vell, vell, vell.   We all vas on earth alretty vonce,
aind it.   [*Children crowd around him, they join hands and
dance around singing until* **Franz** *bumps into* **Holmes.**]

Franz.   Oxcuse me.—

Holmes.   Who are you?

Franz.   I vas a cobbler—yah, de merry cobbler.

Holmes.   A sherry cobbler?

Franz.   No, not a sherry cobbler—I rodder have beer.

Holmes.   [*Aside.*]   This Dutchman seems quick witted.   Perhaps he may be useful to me.   [*Aloud.*]   Rather have beer, eh?
Well here's the money to buy it.   [*Tosses coin to* **Franz.**]

Franz.   [*Does not pick up coin.   Aside.*]   I don't like dot
failer.   He's too chenerous.   I pelieve he stole dot quarter.
[*Aloud.*]   Tanks I'm no Wanderbilt and I'm no beggar neider:
When I drink I choose mein own company—yah—I mean dot.
Come, kinder.   [*Begins to sing.   The children join hands with him
and sing and dance down stage.*   **Holmes** *makes an angry
gesture, picks up coin and exits* R. U. E.   *After song* **Franz** *is* C.]
Now, babies, dis is mein birt-day and I took a liddle holiday mid
you once.   I don'd vork eight hours today, nein.

Leila.   What, nine?   Oh, Franz you said no decent man would
work more than eight.

Franz.   Bet your poots, liddle vun, dot's vhot I sait und I mean
dot.

"Eight hours vork, eight hours play.

Eight hours sleep, makes a perfect day."

Dot's my sendimentals.

Flossie.   But you said you would work nine.

Franz.   Vell, vell, vell.   [*Laughs.*]   Yah, dot's a fact, I did say
nein, aber dot means in Cherman not, neider, nicht—kein—not
any.   I don't vork today at all, not any, aber ve hafe a goot time
togedder.   How is dot?

Children.   Splendid.

Edna.   Let's play "puss in the corner."   You're it.   [*Touches*
Franz.]

Franz.   I don't play.   You didn't give me a square show for
mein vite alley—come now—ve cound oud—[*Children surround
him and he does buss. of "counting out."*]

Ane gesacht, gesinder,
Der Sheeny gebrocht der vinder;
Alle gesoak
Der Sheeny vas croak
Alle gesacht, gesinder.

Vell, vell, vell. I'm it anyhow. [Children *laugh with* Franz.]
Now, den, get in your corners and vatch oud. Keep your eyes
open. [*Buss. of "puss in the corner."*] Now den call oud, pussy
vants a cracker and all such things like dot.

Mrs. R. [*Enters from house* R. *standing on steps. Aside.*]
Look at that Dutchman. Look at that Dutchman. Me heart
is scalded wid him, it is be gorra. [*Crosses so that as* Franz *runs
to get into corner he bumps into her and she falls.* Children *run
up to wall at back.*]

Franz. [R. C. *down.*] Oxcuse me. I hope you didn't proke
your bustle.

Mrs. R. [R. *beside stall.*] Broke my bustle is it, you villain.
[*Rises.*] You've broke my heart, so you have. [*Places hand on
small of back as if in pain.*]

Franz. [*Aside.*] Vet a fonny vay de lady prokens her heart,
aind it? [*Goes* L. C.]

Mrs. R. [*Following him.*] Why don't you go to your work,
you lazy good for nothing thing? Sure 'twas the could day for
me whin Dinnis took you in and learned you to cobble, so it was.
Go on to your work, now, and quit this lallygaggin' or be the
powers I'll sell the bench and turn you out of doors, so I will.
[*Going toward house.*]

Franz. Dot's vhat I vant. I bin trying to git avay from you
Mrs. Rifferty aber you don't let me gone. Now I go me oud in
de vide, vide vorld and seek mein fortune like Chach in de been
stalk und liddle poy blue come plow me your clairinette. [*Goes
up with mock emotion.*]

Mrs. R. Sure you don't nade to get mad about it. [*Following
him up.*]

Franz. [*Stops and turns.*] I ain'd mad--I part from you more
in weptness, dan in anger, Mrs. Rifferty. [*Goes up a step or two.*]

Mrs. R. [*Catches his coat tail.*] Not Rifferty. [*Pulls coat
toward* R.] Rafferty. [*Pulls coat toward* L. *swinging him round.*]

Franz. Dot's vhat I said—Rifferty. [*Suddenly dragging coat
tail out of her hands.*]

Mrs. R. Rafferty. [*Stamping.* Franz *comes down.*]

Franz. Oxcuse me, I don'd can spoke Irish; United States
language is all vat I can tackle at von time. Goot pye Mrs.

Rifferty   I neffer will see you again till we meet on dot peautiful shore.   [*Mock emotion, turns to go up stage.* **Children** *run after him catch his hands and coat tails.*]

Children. Oh, Franz don't go.

Mrs. R. Look a here Dutch—don't lave me like this and me a poor lone widdy. [*Takes his arm c. and brings him down.*] Why don't you settle down and get married?

Franz. Porztausand! Vas ist das? Kit married? Ich? [*Makes a break for* L. U. E. **Mrs. R.** *catches him and drags him back.*]

Mrs. R. [L. C.] Here, here, here—ye don't nade to be in such a hurry about it. What *you* want is a sinsible woman, Dutchy, that's come to the years of discretion and not some floighty shlip of a girl that doesn't know her own mind two minutes. [*Persuasively.*]

Franz. Oh! Ish *dot* vhat I vant?

Mrs. R. To be sure it is, you poor ignorant immogrant.

Franz. Thanks. I'm so glad you told me. Because now dat I know vhat I vant, I know vhat I vant; und vhen I know vhat I vant, I aind so likely to get vhat I don'd vant, aind it? [*Sits on Cobbler's bench* R.]

Mrs. R. That's talk. Now go 'long to your work and see if you can think of some foin woman wid a bit of property. Not too young nor yet not too ould, do ye moind—about me own age— Dutchy. [*Very giddy.*]

Franz. [*Aside.*] Oh jiminy beeswax! Dot face vould start a riot. [*Aloud.*] Vell, I think me about dot, aber I don't vork today for dis is mein birthday.

Mrs. R. [*Aside.*] For heaven's sake. This is the second birthday that Dutchman has had in six months.   I wonder how many times a year he got born. [*Ex. into house* R.]

Franz. [*Looking after her.*] Vell, vell, vell! Of I don't skip oud dot old voman marries me sure. I petter elope mit meinself and fool her vonce. I tink me about dot too. [*Goes* c. **Children** *run down to him.*]

Flossy. I'm going home, Franz, I'm so hungry.

Leila. So am I.

Franz. Hungry? Now I tell you vhat. [*Searching in pocket.*] I have ein, zwei, drei nickels. Come we buy something. Vhat vill you have? [*Goes toward fruit stand followed by* **Children.**]

Rosalie. [*Enters* L.]

Flossy. Chewing gum, Tutti Frutti.

Leila. Peanuts.

Flossy. Bananas.

Leila. Oranges.

Flossy. Pop corn.

Leila. Lemonade.

All. And candy, candy, candy, candy. [*Dancing around him.*]

Franz. Stop, stop, stop. Do you tink I vas a farc pank? Come, ve puy someding anybow. How you vas Rosalie? I gife a party today.

Ros. A party.

Franz. Yah, und dese young ladies vas de inwited guests. I vant you to spread oud de finest party you ever spread oud in all your life for tree nickels. I prowide de nickels und you do de rest. [*Gives money to* **Ros.**]

Ros. [*Laughs.*] Well, well, well——

Franz. Hold on—quit dot—

Ros. Why, what's the matter Franz.

Franz. You sait, vell, vell, vell.

Ros. Suppose I did?

Franz. Vell, dot's my trade mark. I get me a patent on it.

Ros. [*Giving candy, fruit, etc. to* **Children.**] I think you're mighty mean about your old party, anyhow.

Franz. You vas mistooken. Dis is a young party, aind it, liddle vuns?

Children. Yes indeed.

Ros. Well, why didn't you invite me?

Franz. [*Conducts her* c. *mysteriously.*] I vould in a minute, Rosy, but Mrs. Rifferty, she gets chealous. Vhen she gets chealous she gets mad and when she gets mad you imachine dere's a political ward meeting proke loose.

Ros. She's an old terror.

Franz. Aber vhen she gets her mad up I don'd vant her to tarry around me. She gives me de earache.

Ros. I don't see what she has against me.

Franz. She says you vas too giddy.

Ros. Oh, the old thing.

Franz. She says you vas flighty in your mind.

Ros. Well, did you ever.

Franz. Yah,—several times alretty vonce; aber, come along Rosalie. She gets mad anyway so we mights as vell have some fun before de oxplosion tooks place. [**Franz and Ros.** *arrange some boxes* L. *and set oul fruit, seating the* **Children** *who eat while the specialties are going on.*]

Ros. I tell you what, children, this is a lovely little party.

Franz. I told *you* what, Rosalie, you vos a lofely little party your ownself.

Ros. Taffy. I'll tell Mrs. Rafferty that and she'll get red headed.

Franz. Oh, but I didn't mean dot. I vos only chokin. You ain'd nice a liddle bit. But say Rosalie, of Rifferty gets any more red headder as she vas now she looks like a torch light procession.

Ros. That head of hers would fry eggs.

Franz. Now, den, kinder, yoost pitch in and have a goot time. [*Here introduce specialties if possible. After specialties* **Franz** *and* **Rosalie** *sit* R. *at cobbler's bench.* **Children** *are* L. *in bunch.*]

Leila. Our Leiber Franz is the loveliest man in the whole world.

Flossy. And he hasn't had one birthday present.

Leila. Come on girls—we'll get him one. [*The* **Children** *all cross* R.] Good bye, Franz.

Children. Good bye, Lieber Franz.

Franz. Vhat? You all vas goin avay mitout vone kiss? Dot's not peesness. [*They all run and kiss him.*]

Children. Good bye, Lieber Franz—good bye. [*Exit* L. I. E. **Rosalie** *crosses and exits* L.]

Franz. [*Plaintive music.*] Bless deir pure liddle hearts. Of ve could only bin kinder alvays dere vould be no need of heaven for all the angels vould be den on earth. Oh, if mein pocket book vas big enough and mein arms vere vide enough to shelter dem all—dere vould not den be vone homeless, unhappy liddle child in all the vide, vide vorld. [*Music changes to lively. Laughter heard off* R. U. E. **Holmes, Stella** *and* **Carlotta** *enter.*]

Stella. It seems such a silly accident to have the heel come off one's shoe. [*They come down* C. *she has* **Holmes'** *arm.*]

Holmes. Most provoking, but fortunately it is not far to the livery barn and once there you can either drive home or to your shoemaker's and repair the damage.

Car. Why there is a cobbler's stall now. [*Motions with parasol.*]

Stella. The very thing. As this is such a quiet street I'll just sit down and have the heel put on.

Holmes. Oh, I don't think I'd do that, Miss Derrom. This cobbler is an insolent fellow—a German.

Stella. Why, he looks like the soul of good nature. I'll try him anyway. [*Comes down.*] Could you nail the heel of my shoe? I caught it in a grating and wrenched it off a few minutes ago. [*Holds out heel.*]

Franz. I tink so if I tried offul hard; but dis is my holiday, lady.

Stella. But you would oblige me so much. Won't you?

Franz. Sure, mitout the slightest hesitations. I vouldn't see a sweet liddle foot like dot go mitout a heel, not for anytings. Vait, I get you a chair.

Stella. Don't trouble, this box will do very nicely. [*Franz gets chair, she sits and takes off shoe*].

Franz. [*Takes off coat and lays it before her, puts on apron.*] Put your foot on dot, lady, and den you don't took cold from de chilly pavement.

Stella. Thank you.

Franz. Vait. Maybe I have a shoe you can shlip on. [*Picks up several men's shoes, baby shoes, etc.*] You could shlip dot on, aber you get lost. Plenty men's shoes, boy's shoes—horse shoes. [*Holding up a horse shoe, laughs.*] Vell, vell, vell, I'm afraid I can't fit you. [*Goes to work on shoe.*]

Stella. Never mind. I am very comfortable as it is.

Car. [c. *with* **Holmes.**] While you are having your shoe mended, Mr. Holmes and I will take a little stroll, if you don't mind, Stella.

Stella. Not in the least, only don't be gone too long for my heart is set on trying that new horse this morning. He is such a lovely creature, and if he is gentle papa has promised to buy him for me.

Holmes. Then, for ten minutes, au revoir. [*Raises hat.*]

Car. [*Aside to* S.] And be sure you don't fall in love with your handsome cobbler.

Stella. What nonsense. [*They laugh.* **H.** *and* **C.** *exit* L. 1. E.]

Franz. Dot shoe was made in Paris, ain't it?

Stella. Yes, I bought them when I was there, last winter.

Franz. I vas in Paris vonce, mit mein uncle, he vas a great man, mein uncle, he invented a new way to kill peoples. [*Working on shoe.*]

Stella. Why, surely he isn't an executioner?

Franz. Oh, no lady, he's a Cherman chendleman.

Stella. You misunderstand. I meant his business.

Franz. Oh, yah, he's a skientific.

Stella. A what?

Franz. Skientific man. He's de man what invented a new kind of gun powder which kills a hundred mans every lick and dere's so liddle smoke you can see dem all go dead pefore your werry eyes. Bismarck won't have anytings to do mit mein uncle's gun powder, so he gets mad and goes to France mit it. Dot's how I go to Paris mit mein unkel.

Stella. It is a beautiful city.

Franz. Yah, aber you can't *eat* a city   Me und mein uncle ve nearly starved to death.   At last I get so hungry I make complaintment and mein uncle vhip me, den I get me mad and run away to America mit a sailing wessel.

Stella. And weren't you grieved to leave your brothers and sisters?

Franz. [*Puts down shoe emotionally.*] I had no bruder, lady. Aber I had a liddle schweester vonce, a peaudiful liddle schwees ter, which I loved more dan meinself.   She had such lovely big blue eyes, and hair like sonnenschein and she vas a goot girl, lady, as pure in heart as de Edelweiss which blooms in de snowy Alpine passes.   Oh, mein liebe Gretchen, mein liebe Gretchen. [*Emotional.*]

Stella. And your liddle Gretchen is dead?   Poor fellow!

Franz. Yah, lady, *mein* liddle Gretchen is dead [*Intensely, leaning toward her*] Aber dere lives anoder Gretchen, which is no more my liddle schweester—which vas enticed away von her home by a rascal and which brought shame and sorrow on her old uncle and her bruder.   Dot ish why I come bei America vhen I run avay.   Dot villain vas an American which disgraced mein schweester. [*Raising voice. Rises dramatically.*] And vone day vhen ve meet, by Gott, I kill him! [*Pauses, overcome*] Oxcuse me lady, vhen I tink about Gretchen, I forget meinself. [*Drops into seat and covers his face with his hands.*]

Stella. Who was this wretch?   What was he like?

Franz. I did never see him.   Mein uncle sent me to school, and vhile I vas avay dis all did happen.   But his name ish Maurice Stanton, and de day I meet him, he dies.

Stella. How is it, then, with your education that you follow the lowly calling of a shoemaker.

Franz. [*Hammering nails into shoe. Plaintive music.*] I tell you lady.   Vhen I arrived in America I can't spake vone vord of United States language, and I go to Memphis.   Den I come to Noy Orleans and vander aboud de streets, hungry and tired mitout a cent and at last de man vich lived here gives me something to eat and a place to sleep.   Vell, I am no beggar, so I try to help him mit de shoes and by and by he goes dead.   Den his vitve tells me I should go on mit der peesness and so I do, to save up money to help me hunt down Maurice Stanton.   Dere shoe is finished. Dot heel don't come off again mit a hurry, I bet you.   Vait, I putton him up. [*Buttons her shoe. Music stops.*]

Stella. Your sad story has interested me very much, Mr.—— Mr.—

Franz. Yah, Mister, dot's all right.

Stella. But what is your name?

Franz. Franz. Leiber Franz, de babies call me because I play mid dem and dey lofe me.

Stella. Well, Mr. Franz. I hope if you ever meet that wretch, you will stop short of killing him. He richly deserves such a fate but they would hang you for it.

Franz. [*Dramatic music.*] Lady, I vas so disgusted mit life dat I have no friends, no companion, except de children. Dey vould not miss me for long, so if de bullet from mein pistol ever finds Maurice Stanton's false heart, its twin vill find de vay to mine a minute later. [*Music stops.*]

Stella. [*Going c.*] Nonsense, Mr. Franz, you must not give way to such morbid thoughts as these. Believe me, life is well worth living if we strive to be useful to other people. You must rouse your ambition now that you have conquered our language and put your education to a better use than this. How much do I owe you? [*Opening pocket book.*]

Franz. Oxcuse me lady, not vone cent. [*Bowing and steps back.*]

Stella. But I insist. [*Following him as he backs away.*]

Franz. Und I insist. I charge only ven I work; dis vas a pleasure.

Car. [*Enters L. 1. E. with Holmes.*] Are you ready dear?

Stella. Yes it is all finished. [*To F.*] As you will not accept payment for this I shall call tomorrow and leave my order for a pair of riding boots, so good morning Mr. Franz, and many thanks. [*Rejoins C. and H. exit L. U. E.*]

Franz. [*Goes up, watches her off--sighs.*] Vhat you vant is a voman wich has come to de years of discretion like Rifferty, bah! Rifferty, you vas a tam fool. Vhat I vant is a girl like dot vone. [*Comes down to stall.*] Franz, old feller, vhat is de matter mid you? Has dot wicked liddle devil Cupidity been playin' bow and arrow mit your heart? Vell, vell, vell, dot's fonny peesness too, ain't it? [*Takes mirror and looks into it.*] You, a cobbler, mit not two ten cent pieces to play peek-a-boo mit each other fallin' lofe mit a high toned girl like dot? I vas ashamed of you meinself. I thought you had more sensibilities. Franz, I vas sorry to speak harsh to you, mein boy, but to be gandid, you vas like Rifferty—anoder tam fool.

Children. [*Enter L. 1. E. with old rag doll wrapped up in paper.*]

Leila. Come on girls—Now Tottie, you carry it and I'll give it to him.

Flossy. Awe, I want to give it to him.

Leila. Me too.

Flossie. But I've known him the longest and love him the most.

Leila. No you don't. I love him bigger than a street car.

Flossie. Well, I love him bigger than a brick house, so there. It was mine first anyway.

Leila. Well, we'll both give it to him.

Franz. Hello! kinder. You come all pack again vonce? [Children *cross to him. They stop and whisper.*]

Leila. You say it.

Flossie. No, you say it, go on—

Leila. We have brought a present for our Leiber Franz' birthday. [Tottie *hands parcel.*]

Franz. Vell, vell, vell! How did you guess it vas mein birtday? hah? [*Goes* c. *and sits down on stage.* Children *sit around him.*] Vell now, let us look at der presentiment. [*Unwraps doll.*] Splendit. Choost the very ting I vanted. I sait to meinself only last night I vish dose liddle ladies should know tomorrow vas mein birt-day for den perhaps dey might make me a presentiment mit a peautiful doll. Ain't it a dandy? Look at de chuvenile expression in dot eyes, and dose mouth. She's a beaut. Dot's what. [*Rises.*] Vell, I tank you vone and all for dis peautiful gift and I insure you dot dis is de proudest moment of mein existence. [*Kisses all the children.*] Now I tell you vat, ve have a little song and den I dress me up fine and we take der dolly to play in de park. [*Song. After song clamor heard off* L. U. E. *shouts and sound of horse galloping. Hurry music.*]

Franz. Stop here, kinder. [*Crowd them down* R. *in corner.*] Dot sounds like a runavay. [*Runs up to* L. U. E..] Ach Himmel! It is a runavay. [*Horse effect worked closer, cries without of* "stop him," "stop him" *and clamor worked up.* **Mrs. R.** *enters from house* R. **Ros.** *enters* L. *They run up.* **Bob** *enters* R. U. E. [*All worked very quick.*] Mien Gott! It is dot young lady! [*Rushes off* L. U. E. *A cheer is heard off joined by those upon stage.*]

Mrs. R. Lord preserve us, he's killed. [*Runs off* L. U. E. *with* **Bob.**]

Ros. He has stopped the horse and saved the lady, but he must be trampled to pieces. They pick him up—they are carrying him here. [**Bob** *and* **Holmes** *carry* **Franz** *on. He is gastly white with blood on his face and forehead.* **Stella** *supported by* **Mrs. R.** *and* **Charlotta** *follows. They lay* **Franz** *down.* **Stella** *supports his head, others form picture. Plaintive music. Slow curtain.*]

Bob.—Holmes.　　　　　**Charlotta.**　　　　**Mrs. Rafferty.**

Franz—Stella.

Rosalie.

Children.

[*Note. The success of this climax depends in a great
measure upon the noise and excitement worked up off the stage,
which should last fully 30 seconds, faint at first and growing
louder and louder until a loud crash is heard immediately after
Franz rushes off. Then the cheer is heard. This should be
carefully rehearsed with the music if possible.*]

ACT II.

[*Sitting room at* **Mrs. Rafferty's.**　*Table* c. *against flats—table
down* R. *Chair on each side of table. Sofa* L. *partly broken.
No carpet. Old and much worn furniture.* **Mrs. R.** *enters at
rise. Door* L. *in flat.*]

Mrs. R.　So he's not up yet the darlin' man. [*Listening at door*
R. *in flat.*]　I can hear him breathing. [*Comes down a little.*]
Well, if I loiked him before, sure I'm dead stuck on
him now and I'd capture him too if it wasn't that he's bloind
mad in love wid Miss Derrom, forward chit that she is. [*Go to
door* R. *in flat and knocks, calls.*]　Franz—are ye roisin'?　Are
ye roisin. I say?　Sure there's a gintleman to see you.

Franz.　[*Without.*]　Vell, show him up—I bin dere directly.

Mrs R.　Sure, tis inundated he'll be wid visitors this day for
'tis the first toime the docthor ud let him resave. [*Goes to* D. L. F.
and opens it.]　Come in sor—come in. [*Follows* **Findham** *down.*]

Find.　[*Enters* D. L. F.]　Ah—the sumptuous apartments of the
young German American hero. [*Down* C.]　Madam, have a card,
you may need something in my line. [*Presents card.*]　Detective
work of all kinds done with neatness, rapidity and secrecy.　Mat-
rimonial troubles a specialty.　Don't happen to have any matri-
monial troubles on hand just now, do you?

Mrs. R.　[R. C. *looking at card. Aside.*]　The man ud talk a
hole through an iron pot.　Sure he has more cheek than Paddy
Murphy's pig. [*Aloud.*]　No I have not. But I wish to the
Lord I had, anything is better than bein' a lonely widdy woman.

Find.　Cheer up, madam, cheer up!　While there's life there's
hope and a fine looking lady like you has but to choose her mate,

lead him to the hymeneal alter and make him her own.

Mrs. R.   Yis, first catch your hare; then cook it. [*Crosses* L.]

Find.   [C.]   You are facetious, madam. I have no hair. [*Raises hat.*] I haven't enough to swear by, let alone cook. Besides, I object to cooked hair on principle. In the hash foundry which I infest, we have it served up every morning in the codfish balls.

Mrs. R.   If you'd only give your mouth a rest and your brain a chance, you'd see that the hair you mane and the hair I mane is two different koind of hairs. But I can't stop here blatherin' wit you all day. Sit down and take a sate till he comes. [*Exit* D. L. F.]

Find.   Charming person, charming woman—a trifle tart perhaps, acid in fact, but so's a lemon, and a lemon's a darned good thing too—in its place. Her place is wrestling pots. [**Franz** *enters* D. R. F.] Ah! Goot day, goot day, Mr. Franz, I believe? Charmed to see you—allow me to assist you. [*Helps him to chair by table down* R&]

Franz.   Chendly, chendly, mein freund, mein body is all feet prints where dat horse stepped on me. Oh! Oh! [*Sits.*] I feel me like a church vindow—all pains and no putty.

Find.   [*Draws chair up.*]   Now to begin, your name is Franz.

Franz.   Yoh—dot's me. I wish I was somebody else.

Find.   First name. [*Takes out note book and pencil.*]

Franz.   Franz.

Find.   Oh, Franz, Franz. Peculiar name. Puts me in mind of Ylang Ylang or Schmitt Schmiddt. [*Writes in note book.*] Native of Germany?

Franz.   No. I vas Irish. Can't you tell dot by mein accentuation?

Find.   Ha, Ha! Good, capital. Father and mother living?

Franz.   [*Rises.*]   Oho! I'm onto you now, Peat tie. You vas vone of dem newspaber fellers which interviews peoples and when a man says to you, "I vont say vone vord" you print half a column vhat he *didn't* say and make a monkey of him. Look at de tings dey had aboud me in dot pabers alretty vonce—goot bye—I meet you again in a hundred years, if not later. [*Goes up.*]

Find.   [*Follows him and bars* D. R. F.]   You are wrong. When I was younger and wickeder, I confess it with shame, I *was a* newspaper reporter. But now, now, I am a detective.

Franz.   [*Aside.*]   I tink dot fellers crazy. [*Aloud.*]   So you was a detectif? Vell, vhat you vant?

Find.   [*Leading* **Franz** *down.*]   I am on the trail of one of the greatest confidence men of the age.

Franz.   You come de wrong place. Better you try next door.

[Gets away from F.]

Find. That man's name is——

Franz. I don't vant to know his name—I'm not him and dot settles it.

Find. But I just want to talk to you a little——

Franz. Go avay—go avay—you vill talk me to death.

Find. Well, but——

Franz. I don't care a continental who you butt or what you butt, you old billy goat.. Only leave me alone.

Find. Very well, young man you'll be sorry for this. I've tried to serve you and you wouldn't let me. Now serve yourself. Good day. *[Exit D. L. F. angrily.]*

Franz. Good day.

Find. *[Opens door and sticks head in.]* Good day. *[Louder.]*

Franz. Good day. *[Much louder. Repeat this three or four times. Comes down.]* Oh, go to der teuffful! Chiminy beeswax. how sick and lonesome I feel—I vant someting, aber, I don't know vedder it's de pain killer oder de fool killer. *[Sits in arm chair.]*

Mrs. R. *[Enters D. L. F.]* And how are you feeling this morning, Franz?

Franz. I'm feeling all over bandages and arnica and feetprints.

Mrs. R. *[Comes down R.C.]* Tis a cruel bruisin' you got, but you're in luck to be alive.

Franz. I vouidn't bet on it.

Mrs. R. Oh, if you only had a woife to take care of ye now! Why don't ye make up your moind and be done wid it?

Franz. I tell you, Mrs. Rifferty, I have so much mind it can't be made up in a hurry, but I tink about it sometimes.

Mrs. R. And do I ever come into your thoughts whin you think, Franzy?

Franz. *[Aside.]* Franzy. *[Disgusted.]* Oh, if I only had an ax!

Mrs. R. What's that you say, Franzy?

Franz. Frequently, Mrs. Rifferty, frequently.

Mrs. R. Thin take me Franz, me darlin' man. I'm yours. *[Kneels.]*

Franz. You come into mein head at night time in mein dreams.

Mrs. R. *[Aside.]* The dear man, he dreams about me. *[Rises.]*

Franz. Yah. I have de night horses. Rifferty, you vas a crank—I don'd vas looking for a vife and grand modder combined.

Mrs. R. Grandmother! Oh, ye Dutch emigrant! If it wasn't

for your helpless condition, I'd scratch your eyes out. [*Going
D. L. F. T.*] Grandmother, oh, the bliggard. [*Exit D. L. F.*]

Franz. Vell, I guess dot seddles it and I get me fired, I go
pack up mein bundle and prepare to move on. [*Limps to D. R. F.
exit.*]

Mrs. R. [*Without.*] No sor, the Colonel isn't here yet but the
Dutchman's in the front room if you want to see him.

Holmes. [*Knocks at door and enters with* **Bob.** D. L. F.] Not
here. So much the better, for now I can finish what I was telling you.

Bob. Sholy, sah. [*They come down C. Franz opens D. R. F.
cautiously.*]

Holmes. [*Sits L. on sofa.*] From what I have learned from
Miss Derrom, this young German is the very boy who was re-
ported among the victims of yellow fever at Memphis. At any
rate the story he told her tallies remarkably well with young
Altenheim's history. [**Franz** *is listening at D. R. F.*] If he *is*
Altenheim, he must be put out of the way.

Bob. [L. C. *laughs.*] Why pshaw! Let me get him down
along de levee and dey'll be a cuttin' match in full swing so
sudden he'll nevah know how it commenced. [*Draws white
handled razor from his hip pocket.*] One quick slash wid dis
across de gemmen's neck, a splash, and by de time de police get
dar he'll be floating down de Mississip' wiv his froat cut.

Franz. [*Aside.*] Vhat a nice places dot levee is for me—to
keep avay from. [*Exit door R. F.*]

Holmes. [*Startled.*] What was that? [*Goes up a few steps.*]

Bob. Somebody in de naixt room, I reckon. [*Points D. R. F.*]

Holmes. The cobbler, I suppose. Now hurry to Col. Derrom's
office with the note I gave you.

Bob. Yes sah.

Holmes. You're quite sure that Miss Derrom has been coming
here?

Bob. Dead sho'. I hung around like you told me and I see
her myself. Reckon she must be stuck on dis yer Dutchman.

Franz. [*Without.*] Mrs. Rifferty—Oh Mrs. Rifferty.

Holmes. Quick—clear out and I'll see what information I can
pick out of this fellow.

Bob. Yes, sah. [*Going D. L. F.*] Oh, when I get him down on
de levee. [*Exit chuckling.*]

Franz. [*Opening D. R. F.*] Mrs. Rifferty, vhy don'd you answer
me vhen I—— Oh, oxcuse me—I tought you vas Rifferty. Vell,
vell, vell. [*Laughs.*]

Holmes. She was here a few minutes ago but left me alone to
wait for you.

Franz. Oh dot's it. [*Limps down to arm chair* R.]

Holmes. [*Down* R. C.] You seem to mend slowly after the accident.

Franz. I vas so much broken up dere vas a good deal to mend. Oh, oh [*Sits.*]

Holmes. I have called to thank you for saving the life of the young lady I am engaged to and to ask you to accept this as a slight earnest of what I intend to do for you when you get well. [*Gives money.*]

Franz. [*Aside.*] A slight earnest of vhat he vill do for me when I get well—down by der levee. [*Pauses.*] Twenty dollars. I buy me a gun mid dot. [*Aloud.*] Tanks! You're a chendelman. [*Aside.*] I'm a liar.

Holmes. Miss Derrom tells me you came to this country on board the Yungfraw.

Franz. Yah—dot's so.

Holmes. Then, thank heaven, I have at last found the nephew of my old friend, Professor Altenheim. [*Tries to shake hands.*]

Franz. Oxcuse me. [*Puts hands behind him.*] You vas mistooken.

Holmes. What! Aren't you Franz Altenheim?

Franz. Nein. Dot poor failer vent dead mit fever in Memphis. I vas mit him at de time and pooty nearly vent dead meinself.

Holmes. Then your name is——

Franz. Franz Dittenhopper. [*Crosses* L.]

Holmes. Oh—I thought that your uncle was my friend Professor Altenheim, the chemist of Berlin.

Franz. Vell, vell, vell. Mistakes vill happen in de best regulated families. I tell you how it vas. Poor Franz's onkel and mein onkel vas both chemists—dey vas chums. Dey both had a nephew—dot vas me and poor Franz vich vent dead, and ve vas chums too.

Holmes. Oh, that was it! Then you and Franz emigrated together?

Franz. Yah—and den poor Franz he emigrated mitout me. [*Points upward.*] Or else—[*Points downward.*]

Holmes. [*Going* R. *Aside.*] Is the fellow lying or not? He seems too simple to have invented this story and besides he has no grounds for suspicion. [*Aloud.*] Then you are able to prove that Franz Altenheim is dead. Will you make an affidavit?

Franz. Alfred David. Is he a Cherman, too?

Holmes. No, no—I mean a sworn statement that Franz Altenheim is dead. I want to send it to his uncle, the Professor, so as to set his mind at rest.

Franz. Dot vouldn't give him no rest. He vouldn't pelieve me on oath.

Holmes. Oh, yes he will! In a case like this it will be a satisfaction to him to know the truth.

Franz. Oh vell, I schwear to anyting you vant, vhen I get better. [*Sits* L. *on sofa.*]

Holmes. Thanks. Well, I must leave you now, but I will call again. Good bye. If you need money just let me know and you shall have it. [*Goes* D. L. F. *Aside.*] Everything works like a charm and as soon as I can arrange proofs of Gretchen's death that will look satisfactory to the authorities, I shall marry Stella and start for Germany on my wedding trip and claim this fortune. [*Exit.*]

Franz. [*Limps to* D. L. F. *looks out, closes door.*] Dot failer's a villain. [*Coming down.*] I wonder vhat he's up to, anyhow? Vhy for does he vant me dead? I find me dis out pooty quick and den, bezoof! Bzip! I knock his eye oud. [*Takes arm out of sling, jumps, etc.*] Dey tink I vas offul sick, but I ain't. De reason vat I get petter so slow is because Stella comes no more after I get me vell, vonce. I vish I neffer *could* get vell if she would only come and see me every day. [*Sits in arm chair* R. *Knock heard* D. L. F.] Choust vat I oxpected—here comes Rifferty to bounce me. [*Calls.*] Come in. [*Aside*] Und I go out sure.

Ros. [*Enters with* Children, D. L. F.] Oh, you poor fellow! How sick you look.

Children. [*Crowd around him, kiss him, etc.*]

Franz. Und, oh, how sick I feel! But I vas offul glad to see you all.

Leila. And we are glad to see our Lieber Franz.

Flossie. We are so sorry you are sick.

Franz. Yah. I vas sorry meinself.

Leila. [*Runs to door and returns with big bouquet of weeds, leaves, etc.*]

Ros. The children have been wild to see you, but Mrs. Rafferty declared you were nearly dead and wouldn't let us in till today. The old dragon.

Leila. But this morning we all went out to the park and picked this bouquet for you. [*Gives him bouquet.*]

Flossie. They are mostly weeds, but they were the best we could get. You don't mind, do you Franz?

Franz. [C. *with* Children *around him.*] Mind! Gott pless your dear liddle hearts! Sooner I would have dot boweue, picked mit your lovely liddle hands, dan de most peaudiful roses dat ever decked a royal reception room. I tink it's lofely and I tink you vas the loveliest babies in the world. Vell, vhat you bin doin' since I bin sick? [*Gives bouquet to* Ros. *who puts it in vase on table* c.]

Ros. Oh, they've played around the fruit stand and I've been giving them dancing lessons.

Franz. So! I must see dem dance once.

Flossie. We've learned some new songs too.

Ros. Oh, but we musn't dance or make a noise here. It might be bad for Franz.

Franz. Vall, I run my chances on dot—come babies, you come and sit mit Franz while Rosalie gives an imitation of dot Quaker girl which goes dancing crazy when she hears music. [**Children** *go* r. *and group around* **Franz.** **Rosalie** *hangs her head and does bashful buss. These lines are omitted if* **Ros.** *does not dance. Or a song for* **Franz, Rosalie** *and the* **Children** *may be introduced, after which* **Rosalie** *and* **Children** *exit. Door* L. F.]

Mrs R. [*Enters* D. L. F.] Oh yoi're here, are ye? Well, there's a wumin to see you. [*Remains at door.*]

Franz. [*Aside.*] I pet it's der wash lady and I haven't a cent. [*Pause.*] Aber I have, though. [*Takes money from pocket.*] Mein gracious—I nearly did forget dose twenty dollars. [*Aloud.*] Send her up. [*Sits in arm chair* R.]

Mrs. R. And a brazen piece she is to go runnin' after a man every day in the week. Sure, I'll run after *no* man if I *niver* get married. [*Exit* D. L. F.]

Franz. I vish she'd quit chasin' me. Now for de vash lady.

Stella. [*Enters* D. L. F. *She has small basket in hand.*]

Franz. [*Without turning his head.*] Vell, I hope you found dot stocking and mein odder hankerchief. Dis pessness of tryin' to get on mit vone hankerchief a veek is played out. Have you change for a twenty? [*Holds out note.*] Vell, are you dumb? [*Turns and sees* **Stella.** *Rises.*]

Stella. [*Laughs. Comes down* L. C.] Why, Franz—did you take me for your washwoman? [*Laughs and goes up.*]

Franz. Don't laugh—Miss Derrom—I vas so ashamed mit meinself I don't know what to do—Oh! I'm a chump—a chackass a mool—you ought to get mad vonce and gone avay.

Stella. [*Putting basket on table up* C.] Why Franz, you did nothing to make me angry—you could not anger me by anything you might do. [*Coming down.*]

Franz. I tink I could and maybe I try sometime.

Stella. You may try, but you will not succeed. You saved my life at the risk of your own when scores of other men shrank from the maddened horse in terror—when Morris Holmes, my affianced husband, sought his own safety by leaping from the vehicle and left me to my fate.

Franz. Oh—dot vas notting—notting at all. De next time you vant a runaway stopped, yoost send for me. [*Sits in arm chair* R.]

Stella. You always make light of what you do, but I do not. Well, how are we today? [*Goes to table, brings grapes, etc. from basket.*]

Franz. Dis end of de combination is sorry to say he feels much better.

Stella. Feel much better and are sorry for it?

Franz. Yah—dot's funny aint it?

Stella. Very odd.—I don't understand it at all.

Franz. Vell, I oxplain. No, I better not—you get mad.

Stella. Indeed I'll not. [*Comes down.*] But come, have some of these grapes and a glass of wine. It will do you good. [*Offers them to him,* R. C.]

Franz. Oh, vhy can't I be sick forever and ever, amen?

Stella. Why, what odd things you are saying today! Why should you wish that?

Franz. Oh, vell—because—

Stella. Because what?

Franz. You don't get mad?

Stella. I promise not to.

Franz. So help you, Chimy Chonson?

Stella. [*Laughs.*] Upon my word.

Franz. Say, did it look like rain when you come in?

Stella. Not a bit. [*Aside.*] Oh, how provoking he is. [*Aloud.*] Come now tell me why you don't want to get well.

Franz. Oh, I don't like to. You'll get your mad up sure.

Stella. No I wont. Now tell me.

Franz. Vell—vell—oh say—Holmes was here today.

Stella. Oh, bother Mr. Holmes! I hate him.

Franz. Chiminy beeswax—vhat a nice wife you'll make him!

Stella. I won't. I'll not be his wife at all. Papa forced me into this hateful engagement but I'll break it off. I'll never marry him.

Franz. [*Rises.*] Oho-o o! [*With long drawn rising and falling inflexion.*]

Stella. Now if you don't tell me this minute why you don't want to get well I'll go right straight home and never come back.

Franz. Dot's the reason. You guessed it in de first flop out of de box.

Stella. . You seem determined not to tell me.

Franz. [*With pathos.*] Why for should I? You told me. Vhen I get vell you go away and I never see you any more, because you are a grand lady and I -[*Pause.*] am only a poor cobbler. [*Bends over arm chair with his back to audience.*]

Stella. Franz. [*Touches him on shoulder.*] Franz you must not think so meanly of me as that -- I owe you a debt that nothing can repay-- I will --always be glad - to see you [*Goes l.. aside.*] Beware little girl--beware--you are getting into very deep water a little more and you would have been carried off your feet that time.

Franz. I don't know if I always will be glad to see you.

Stella. You are very contradictory. Why not?

Franz. I'm scared.--I had a schweetheart vonce in Chermany. Dot's de reason.

Stella. Oh! You had. [*Tossing her head angrily.*]

Franz. I told you I make you mad vonce. Vhat you get mad about?

Stella. Because——

Franz. Because vhat?

Stella. Because you never told me before.

Franz. You never gave me de chance. But come—ve talk about sometings else! De babies vas here today and Rosalie. Oh! dey looked splendid and brought me dot lofely bocwue. Dey made it demselves. Yah.

Stella. The dear little soulds. That just reminds me, Miss Lemoine wants you to bring them all to her house on the river as soon as you get well enough. Do you think their mothers will let them come?

Franz. Dey ought to. I've been actin' as deputy nurse girl to de crowd long enough.

Stella. Then I'll let you know what day she appoints. *Now Franz, I want you to sing me one song and then I must go.*

Franz. *I'll sing you a new vone vat you never heard before.* Vhat a strange tings is society—ain it? [*She gets a low stool at his feet.*]

Stella. A very strange thing. It puts up barriers between people sometimes which separate them almost as effectually as death itself.

Franz. Yah—it was like a sea mitout a boat—like a river mitout a bridge.

[*Song, "Across the Sea."*]

[*After song* **Stella** *is weeping. He pauses and looks at her. The lines in Italics are not spoken when song is omitted.*]

Franz. Vhy, Miss Derrom—vhat ish der matter? Vas ist? Stella tell me. Vhat makes you cry?

Stella. [*Sobbing.*] You—you were—thinking about—about your sweetheart in Germany. [*Goes* L. C.]

Franz. [*Following her.*] You vas mistooken—it vas about a social sea which stretches so far between me and de only woman which lives in mein heart—So far, far avay it stretches dat if I should hold out mein hands she vould not see dem—if I should say "I love you—I love you" she dare not hear.

Stella. But if she did see—and if she did hear, Franz?

Franz. Aber she does not; she never vill.

Stella. She does—she does. [*He puts his left arm around her.*]

Franz. Mein gracious! How did all dis happen? Maybe you better use de odder arm too. [*Takes arm* R. *out of sling and puts it around her also.*] You might fall and hurt yourself.

Stella. Why, I thought your shoulder was so terribly sprained. [*They cross* R.]

Franz. So it vas—a liddle. I make believe to be worse dan I am so you wouldn't quit comin' so quick.

Stella. Oh, you fraud!

Holmes and Col. *Enter quietly* D. L. F. **Mrs. R.** *follows them. Music, p. p.*]

Franz. Aber you seem to like me pretty vell. [*Kisses her.*]

Holmes. There, Colonel—you see for yourself.

Col. [*Up* C.] What is the meaning of this, Stella, that I find you, a Derrom, in the arms of this cobbler? [*Comes down.*]

Stella. [*Down* R. C.] Cobbler, he may be, father, but he is a gentleman and a brave man and I love him.

Holmes. [*Coming down.*] So, Miss Derrom, you stand there with my engagement ring flashing on upon your finger and have the hardihood to confess your love for this low fellow to my very face. [L. C.]

Stella. [*Takes off ring and throws it at him.*] Take your hateful ring and your freedom with it, Mr. Holmes, but do not dare again to insult the man whose gallant bravery showed you to be the poltroon and coward that you are. [*Drops down to* R. *corner.*]

Holmes. [*Music f. In a rage.*] You are a woman and may insult me with impunity. [*To* **Franz.**] But as for you, I'll—— [*Takes a step towards* **Franz** *threatening.*]

Franz. Stop where you are—you forgot dat dis room is mein house. I order you to leave it. [*Points to door, picture. Music. ff.*]

Curtain.

[*Second picture.* **Franz** *in armchair* R. *with arms over table and head resting on arms.* **Holmes** *up at door* L. F. *with arm around* **Stella** *as if dragging her off. She is turned looking back at* **Franz.** **Col,** *up stage pointing to door as if ordering her off.*]

ACT III.

[*Garden scene. Bench down* R. *Set as elaborately as possible. At rise* **Stella** *and* **Carlotta** *enter* L. U. E. *and come down to bench* R.]

Stella. [*Speaks as she enters.*] It is going to be a lovely evening for your party, dear.

Carlotta. Charming. Now I wonder whether I have forgotten anything? Let me see! The sandwiches, ice cream, candy, fruit, music, yes, everything is ready and we only wait the return of the yacht.

Stella. It was so kind of you, dear, to give the children a happy evening. [*Sets on bench* R.]

Charlotta. [*Laughs.*] Yes—and you another opportunity to see Franz. By the way, mama insisted on inviting Mr. Holmes, what will you do?

Stella. Ignore him, my dear, as usual. It appears that he has fallen heir to an enormous fortune in Germany, and that is the reason papa insists on my marrying him, but I wouldn't be his wife—no, not if he were as rich as the lottery company.

Charlotta. There. I knew I had forgotten something!

Stella. What is it?

Charlotta. Flowers for the supper table. Come, we will just have time to arrange them before they arrive. [*Exit* R. I. E.]

Holmes. [*Enters with* **Findham,** R. U. E.] This news is important, if true.

Find. [C. *He shows that he has been drinking.*] If true! Oh Lord! The idea of I. L. Findham, the fox, the ferret, the sit-up-all-night-we-never-sleep private detective, making an error or turning in a faked report. Mr. Holmes, you have done me wrong, sir. My professional pride is touched on the raw and my sensitive feelings are lacerated. Allow me to present an itemized bill to date and respectively withdraw from the case. [*Hands paper.*]

Holmes. [L. C.] Don't be an ass. [*Refuses paper.*]

Now let us see what there is in this. What does the woman call herself?

Find. Mrs. Maurice Stanton.

Holmes. How do you know this?

Find. Because she applied to my landlady for work. I was in the next room and the moment I heard her speak that name I glued my ear to the keyhole.

Holmes. What else did you learn?

Find. That she has traced her child from New York to New Orleans and is now compelled by lack of funds to drop the search for a time.

Holmes. This is bad, very bad. My friend Stanton is away from the city at present and I don't know how to communicate with him. It is of the utmost importance to keep the child out of the mother's clutches till the divorce case is tried and he is given legal custody. Confound it, I don't know what to do. [*Rises.*]

Find. [*Going L.*] Don't say a word—don't breathe—my think tank is beginning to evolve the solution. I have it. [*Turns.*] Send her some place else before the mother finds her. What's the matter with that?

Holmes. [c.] Everything. To begin with, the people who are caring for her don't know me and wouldn't give her up without a written order from Stanton—perhaps not then.

Find. [L. C.] Steal her—kidnap her—abduct her—run her off.

Holmes. Your think tank, as you call it, has evolved. That is precisely the idea.

Find. Great scheme, great head. Here's success to the scheme, have a nip? [*Takes flask from hip pocket.*]

Holmes. Thanks I never touch liquor.

Find. That's right. Its an awful curse. [*Drinks.*]

Holmes. It can be done tonight quite easily. She is one of the youngsters who is coming here with our cobbler friend. Black Bob has secured the job of running Lemoine's yacht and is to bring the party up here from the city. I will give him the tip to keep steam up and you watch your opportunity to get the child on board and carry her off as soon as it grows dark.

Find. Excuse me. *You* watch *your* opportunity to get the child on board and carry her off. I don't mind laying the plan, but object to turning the trick myself. It's too risky.

Holmes. Nonsense! There is no risk in it at all. Who is there to make trouble? Not the mother, for she doesn't know where the child is and has no money to find her if she did. Cer-

there to make trouble? Not the mother, for she doesn't know where the child is and has no money to find her if she did. Certainly not Stanton, and the people she lives with will be quieted by a letter from him as soon as I can reach him. [*Sits* R.]

Find. You've forgotten the cobbler. He's fond of the kid and will raise the devil the minute she's missed.

Holmes. He can't do anything. You know just as well as I do that the police don't loose any sleep if there's nothing in it for them; and he hasn't a cent.

Find. How about piracy? Running away with a vessel. Don't you know the penalty for piracy? They hang you by the neck from a yard arm till you are dead, dead, dead – three times. Then you are generally defunct. Oh, I'm no pirate. [*Goes* L.]

Holmes. [*Rises and crosses to* F.] That's all right. Lomoine is a friend of mine, in fact he and Derrom are interested in one of my mining enterprises. I'll explain matters after all is over and he will make no trouble. But this is the best argument after all. [*Takes out roll of money.*] 10, 20, 40, 60, 80, $100, and here's another hundred to keep it company.

Find. [*Taking money.*] Your logic is unanswerable. I shall enter in my financial report for tonight. "Business is picking up and money easier. Price of kids advanced with a rush to $200 cash." [*Puts money in pocket. Takes out flask and drinks.*] I shall also remark that whiskey has gone down.

Holmes. See that it doesn't go down too often, for you will need a clear head tonight. [*Going up with* F. *to* L. U. E.] Now that is settled and you'd better come back here as soon as it grows dark. Above all things, don't make yourself conspicuous.

Find. Mr. Holmes, you are once more wrong. The best thing I can do is to make myself extremely conspicuous – by my absence. [*Exit* L. U. E.]

Holmes. [*Coming down.*] So Gretchen has turned up again almost in time to spoil my plan. But forewarned is forearmed, and knowing that she is here, I shall make myself scarce at once. Oh, well, it will only hurry matters, that's all. I must get the mining stock unloaded on Lemoine and Derrom at the best price they will give and start for Germany at once. Now I'd better pay my respects to madam. [*Exit* R. 1. E.]

Find. [*Re-enters* L. U. E. *looks about.*] Oh, he's gone. The chump never told me where he wanted the kid taken to. I'd better wait here till I see him. [*Sits* R. *Takes out money and counts it.*] Correct he didn't even try to pinch a note or give me the double cross. [*Takes out flask.*] He's a gentleman and here's his health. [*Drinks. Holds flask upside down.*] Empty is the [*hic*] cradle. I've got to get that filled. I never travel without a little drop in case of [*hic*] sickness. I'll see him later and find out where he [*hic*] wants me to take the kid. [*Goes* L. U. E. *singing.*] "Where are you going to my little maid?"

"*Where are you going my little maid?*"

"Darned if I know," kind sir she said. [hic] Neither do—do I. [Stella *and* Car. *enter* R. I. E. *and watch him. He turns at entrance, straightens up, raises hat.*] Excuse me—[hic.] Didn't know there were ladies present. Good evening. [*Exits* L. U. E.]

Car.   I wonder what that man was doing in our house?

Stella.   Oh, never mind him. But let's see if the boat is coming. [*They go up and look off* R.]

Car.   I hope no accident has happened. I don't like that new engineer—a colored boy whom papa engaged on Mr. Holmes' recommendation and I don't trust him.

Stella.   [*Coming down with* Carlotta.] Why, what do you dislike about him?

Car.   The mere fact that Holmes got him the place is enough to make me hate him. [*Distant steamboat whistle heard off* R.]

Stella.   Hark—what is that?

Car.   They are coming. [*They look off* R.]

Stella.   Yes, there she comes around the bend. [*They wave handkerchiefs.*] They see us, look, there is Franz in the bow waving his handkerchief to us. [*Distant singing heard off* R. *and noise of tug. Singing comes nearer, whistle heard close.*]

Franz.   [*Enters with* Rosalie *and* Children, R.U.E. *all singing.*] Vell vell, vell—Dese kids vas pretty near gone crazy mit der steamboat. [*They come down,* Children *sit on bench* R. *with* Rosalie.

Car.   [L. C. *To* Stella C.] Oh what a dreadful thing it is to be in love. [Bob *enters* R. U. E. *carries wraps, etc.*]

Car.   Did the Grace act properly, Bob? [*Takes wraps from him.*]

Bob.   Sho'ly Missy. She's a peach, dat's what she is. I'll just go and bank my fire. [*Exit* R. U. E.]

Franz.   [*Takes parcel from* Charlotta.] Yah, dot's mein, Danke schon. I take care of him. [*Exit* L. U. E.]

Car.   [*Aside to* Stella.] I know you are just dying to be alone with him for a few minutes, so I'll take the children and Rosalie and present them to mama. You can follow with Franz, but don't stop too long. [Franz *re-enters.*]

Stella.   [*Aside to* Car.] You're an angel, Lotta, and I'll do as much for you some day.

Franz.   [C.] Vas is dis? Secrets? Come, tell me. Ladies'

secrets vas alvays made to be told.

Car. You will find this one out for yourself in a few minutes. Come children. [**Children** *join her.*]

Ros. [R.] Am I one of the children or one of the folks?

Franz. You have a child's ticket, Rosalie, goot for dis trip only.

Ros. Well, you're traveling on your face and the conductor ought to punch it. [*Goes with* **Charlotta** *and* **Children** *to* R. I. E.]

Leila. [*Hanging back.*] But we want Franz to go too.

Franz. Oh, go vay, Leila, you can't oxpect to bin tied to Franz's apron string all de time. Scoot along now. I choin you later.

Flossie. Well, don't be long.

Leila. No, don't be a minute.

Franz. I von't be a second—[*Aside.*]—quicker dan I can help. [**Car. Ros.** and **Children** *exit*, R. I. E.] Vell.

Stella. Well.

Franz. Is dis mein welcome vhen I haven't seen you for a veek?

Stella. Well, I haven't seen you for a week, either.

Franz. Hah? How *is* dot? I haven't seen *you* for a week and you haven't seen *me* for a veek—mein gracious! Ve haven't seen each odder for two weeks, aint it? How you vas? [*Shakes hands.*]

Stella. I am very glad to see you. What more could you ask?

Franz. Several tings—I show you. [*Throws down parcel.*] One, two, three. [*Holds arms open, catches and kisses her.*] You're "it."

Stella. That's a queer game.

Franz. You like him? We try him again and I'll be "it" next time. One, two, three—[*She turns away*].—vhy—you don't play? Who's de reason?

Stella. I am worried. [*Sits* R.]

Franz. Oh, about dot nice ole chendleman, your fadder. How *is* the old duck anyvay?

Stella. Still angry and trying to force me to marry that wretch, Holmes.

Franz. Aber you von't and he von't vant you to, needer, vhen I find me out a liddle more.

Stella. Why, have you discovered anything new?

Franz. Vell, I should say! You know dot newspaper feller vich vants to print some lies aboud me in de papers and says he is a detective?

Stella. You told me about him.

Franz. He's a willain. He's a freund mit Holmes.

Stella. How did you find this out?

Franz. I skin mein eyes and see him hanging round. Den I follows der detectif and by chimney he meets Holmes on de corner and goes in a saloon mit him. Dey gits acquainted mit each odder rightavay quick.

Stella. They had an appointment.

Franz. No, dey only had beer. Der detectif paid for it and I guess he vent broke. You know dot black and tan vich runs der steam boat?

Stella. You mean Bob?

Franz. Yah, dot's de prize peaudy vich vants to tade me valking on de levee mit a white handled razor. Oh, I'd like to shoot craps mit him—much not.

Stella. Why, Holmes got him his place with Mr. Lemoine.

Franz. [*Whistles.*] Vhat have I struck? A picnic!

Stella. And Mrs. Lemoine has invited Holmes here this evening.

Franz. Vell, if der detectif turns up it makes a nice tree of a kind to draw to.

Stella. I wish I could find out just what Holmes is trying to do.

Franz. I find me out tonight and den I tell you.

Stella. I hope you will. But, dear me, we have been here too long now. [*Rises.*] I must take you to be introduced to Mrs Lemoine, our hostess. Which way shall we go, the long or the short way?

Franz. Better ve go de long vay, ve get dere sooner. De broke» bridge is always on de short cut. [*Exit* R. I. E.]

Holmes. [*Enters* R. 2 E.] I wonder where that nigger is? [*Calls.*] Bob—Oh, Bob.

Bob. [*Off* R. U. E.] Yes sah. Comin' sah. [*Enters.*]

Holmes. How is your steam?

Bob. Just banked de fire, sah.

Holmes. Then you'd better unbank it as quick as you know how. You've got to keep steam up and be ready to start at a moment's notice.

Bob. Where fo' sah?

Holmes. Anywhere away from New Orleans.—Hades, if you like.

Bob. Hades? Whah is dat town, sah? I nevah heard tell of it—nevah.

Holmes. You'll get there bye and bye just the same. There's a child here, that little Leila, who will be the better for a change of air. Findham will bring her on board after dark and you must be ready to cast off and run like a streak of light the moment he does so.

Bob. What'll de boss say?

Holmes. Never you mind the boss, you mind me or it will be the worse for you. If you begin disputing my orders I'll give you away to the police and you'll be a gone coon sure.

Bob. Oh, I wasn't sputin no orders, Master Holmes.

Holmes. I thought you objected to taking the boat.

Bob. Deed no, sah. You keep me out of de penitentiary at Baton Rouge and I'll steal de hull Vicksburg line if you say so—deed I will.

Holmes. That's all right. you know which side of your bread is buttered.

Bob. Reckon I does, sah. [*Exit* L. E. U. *chuckling*.]

Holmes. Confound that Findham—why doesn't he come. [*Goes up*.]

Franz. [*Appears* R. I. E. *Aside*.] Ah, here he vas alretty vonce. Now I vatch him. [*Watches unseen*.]

Holmes. [*Calls*.] Bob, Oh, Bob.

Bob. [*Off* R. U. E.] Yes sah, I's coming sah. [*Re-enters*.]

Holmes. Have you seen anything of Findham? [*They come down*.]

Bob. No, sah. I haint seen hide nor hair of Mistah Findham, sah.

Franz. [*As soon as* Bob *and* Holmes *are down stage sneaks across and hides behind set tree. Aside*.] Findham, dot's der detectif and he can't find him. [*Exit* L. 2 E.]

Holmes. [c.] I can't understand what can have become of him.

Bob. [L. C.] I'll never tell you.

Holmes. There is no time to lose. Leila must be out of New Orleans tomorrow night, for every minute she stays here is a menace to my plans. If Findham has got drunk, and I guess that's what's the matter, we will have to carry this thing through by ourselves.

Bob. Yes sah.

Holmes. I don't wish to be mixed up in the transaction anyway so you must be on the alert. I will place the child in the boat and you can carry her off by yourself.

Bob. Anything you say goes, boss.

Holmes. Now go back to the boat and don't fall asleep. Is steam up?

Bob. It will be in a minute, sah. [*Goes* R. U. E. *as* **Find.** *enters*

L. U. E.] Heah's de gemman now, sah. [*Exit.*]

Find. [*Aside. Hic.*] He's mad. I can see it by the expression of his neck. Brace up, Picey, and have some style about you. [*Braces up to come down as* Holmes *turns, then walks quickly down.*]

Holmes. Well, what do you mean by this?

[Find, *steadying himself at garden seat* R.] Mean by what?

Holmes. Making a beast of yourself as you have done when you have important work on hand.

Find. For the second time today you lacerate my professional feelings with a most [*hic*] a most unjust suspicion. I assure you on the word of an honorable private detective it is the water [*hic*] the rascally water that's to blame.

Holmes. Water, you drunken fool; what has that got to do with it?

Find. Now don't get mad, I'll be all right in a few minutes, my jag always catches me in waves like this. The fact is, the water about here isn't fit to drink, so I was obliged to take something in it to [*hic*] to kill the malaria.

Holmes. Well, you are of no use here, and you'd better go home.

Find. There's no train.

Holmes. Go to a hotel.

Find. There's only one, and it's fuller'n I am.

Holmes. Oh, go to the devil.

Find. Don't believe in him. [*Hic.*] I read Bob Ingersoll. Now don't make any mistake—I'll be all right in a few minutes and I've only got enough on board to give me nerve for the job. I'll carry out my contract, don't you fret.

Holmes. No, I can't trust you. You have that infernal flask and I suppose it is loaded to the muzzle. Give it to me and then I'll be sure of your not growing worse instead of better. Give it to me this minute. [*Drags him* C.] Hand it over.

Find. See here, Holmes, there's only one man living who can look at me in that tone of voice.

Holmes. There is eh! And who is he?

Find. [*Meekly.*] You. Sir. [*Hands flask to* H.] Have you your life insured?

Holmes. No. Why?

Find. You'd better before you tackle that. [*Crosses* L.] Now where am I to take the kid when I get her?

Holmes. Any place you like, only wire me where you are and wait for instructions. Now, no more foolishness.

Find. Won't you give me enough of that dynamite to clear my throat?

Holmes. Not one drop. I'll give this to Bob to keep for you till you are safely on your way.

Find. To Bob! To Bob? [*Goes to* **Holmes** *raises his hand and kisses flask.*] Ta, ta. farewell. I shall never see thee more. alas.

Holmes. Now keep out of sight till they come down here, When they do, watch for a favorable chance to get hold of the child. Bob has his instructions and will be ready to cast off the moment you are on board. [*Goes* R. U. E.]

Find. All right. I'll be on hand just like a sore thumb.

Holmes. Be careful then, no blundering. [*Exit* R. U. E.]

Find. [*Looking after* **Holmes.**] Holmes, you're one of the smartest men on earth--in your mind—you don't beat around the bush, you pluck it up by the roots, you do. You remove the cause to stop the effect and go in for the kind of prohibition that prohibits. [*Takes another flask from pocket.*] But like the other innocent reformers, you didn't calculate on the blind pig. Here's your health Holmesy, old boy. [*Drinks.*] This is a regular kindergarten object lesson on the theory and practice of temperance reform in Iowa. [**Franz,** *enters* L. 2 E. *disguised as a girl.*] I'll get it copyrighted. [*Drinks.*] Now for the kid. No blundering. [*Exit* R. 2 E., *stage darkened.*]

Franz. [*Come down and watches him off.*] Vhat a peautiful load dot feller is gettin'. I vish I had half his complaint. [*Laughter heard off* R.]

Holmes. [*Re-enters* R. U. E.] They are playing hide and seek on the lawn. This is Findham's opportunity, confound him, where is he? [*Sees* **Franz.**] Hello, who are you, my girl? [*Comes down.*]

Franz. [C.] I vas de new nurse girl.

Holmes. [R. C.] Did you meet a young man here just now?

Franz. Vhat you take me for, a masher? I don't go meeting young mans.

Holmes. [*Looks at* **Franz,** *closely. Aside.*] Good heavens. [*Startled.*] She is the very picture of Gretchen! I never saw such a likeness.

Franz. Vhat scares you? I don't bite.

Holmes. Tell me, my girl, where are you from, what is your name?

Franz. Oh, go vay--you vant to flirt mit me.

Holmes. Tell me--what's your name?

Franz. Oh, quit now--don't make a foolishment mit me. I believe you vas a masher your own self.

Holmes. You're a mighty pretty girl, at all events.

Franz. You make me blush when you look at me so funny and say such a tings like dot.

Holmes. [*Goes* R. *Aside.*] That's the idea! If I can only get this girl to impersonate Gretchen it will save all trouble and if she's intelligent enough to be properly coached, none of even Gretchen's intimate friends will suspect the trick. Its worth trying. [*Aloud.*] What did you say your name was? [*Up to Franz.*]

Franz. I didn't say anyting, aber dey call me Lena.

Holmes. And what part of Germany did you come from, Lena?

Franz. Chermany? How did you gess I vas a Cherman?

Holmes. By your beautiful blue eyes and flaxen hair. How long have you been over?

Franz. About seven weeks.

Holmes. Where are you from?

Franz. I vas from Frankfort Sissige.

Holmes. [*Aside.*] Good. So far away from Berlin that it is unlikely any of her friends will see and recognize her. [*Aloud.*] Would you like to have a whole lot of money, Lena?

Franz. Dot's for vhy I come bei America mit a steamboat vich makes me so sick—ach himmel--how I vas sick!

Holmes. Do you know how much a thousand dollars is?

Franz. Silver or gold?

Holmes. You're all right. How long would it take you to save up that much?

Franz. [*Counts on fingers.*] About a hundred years if I'm in luck and get a raise of wages.

Holmes. Come here my girl and I'll tell you how to get it in two months.

Franz. Vhat! A whole tousand dollars? Go vay! [*Crosses* R.] Perhaps you tink I vas a bigger fool dan I look like, aber nicht.

Holmes. I am in earnest. All you have to do is to go back to Germany with me to Berlin and pretend you are somebody else.

Franz. How can I do dot vhen I ain't somebody else?

Holmes. You will have beautiful silk dresses and diamonds.

Franz. And a sealskin cape?

Holmes. Yes, anything you want.

Franz. Mein gracious! How nice I will look in a silk dress mit a long tail and a seal skin cape.

Holmes. You have only to do what I tell you and you shall have all that and more.

Franz. I'll do dot, for diamonds and sealskins. I'd pretend I vas de king of der Cannibal Islands. Say, how large is dem diamonds? So big vie a penny?

Holmes. No, only about as big as a three cent piece.

Franz. Come on, ve start now, right avay, quick. [*Takes his arm and pulls him.*

Holmes. Wait a minute—wait a minute. [*Takes card from case.*] Come to that address tomorrow morning at ten o'clock and I will tell you all about this matter.

Franz. I'll be dere, sure—at ten o'clock. Tomorrow is my day out, yah.

Holmes. Now be careful you don't say a word to anybody about this matter. Don't let anyone see that card. If you do, you'll never wear sealskin and diamonds.

Franz. You pet your neck nobody sees it.

Holmes. Lena, you're a peach. [*Kisses Franz.*]

Franz. Oh, you vicked man. [*Going* R. 2 E. *Aside.*] Now I get mein eyes on de odder villain. Oh, vhat a pair of canary birds dey are. [*Exit.*]

Holmes. She will look like a living picture of Gretchen when she's properly dressed and the fortune is now within my grasp.

Gretchen. [*Enters* L. 1. E. *made up to look as much like* Franz *as possible. Poorly clad and with a shawl thrown over her head.* Holmes *does not hear her but stands looking off* R. 2 E. Gretchen *speaks and he faces her.*] At last! [*Chord. She speaks with a slight German assent.*]

Holmes. [R. C.] My God! Gretchen, you here!

Gret. [C. *Plaintive music.*] Yes, Maurice Stanton, I have found you at last. Look at me, look upon the wreck of your once happy and trusting Gretchen. You wretch! Not content with abandoning me to starve, you have robbed me of my child! Where is she? Tell me where you have hidden her or as sure as there is a heaven above us I will kill you. [*Draws dagger.*]

Holmes. Hush, Gretchen, hush. Do not raise a disturbance here or you will ruin my last opportunity of becoming rich—do you hear me—rich and honestly so.

Gret. Honestly so—you? Bah!

Holmes. I confess I have been wrong—cruel—wicked—but I will atone for the past.

Gret. Atone for the past! You swindler—robber—cheat! Can you atone for my years of agony and grief? For the hunger and cold I have suffered, for the months I passed amid the shrieks and cursings of the maniacs among whom they thrust me after you had torn my little one from me? They said I was mad. [*Crosses* R.]—and I was-driven mad by you, Maurice Stanton.

Holmes. They poisoned my mind against you and I believed you false, Gretchen. That is why I took her from you. When I discovered the truth I sought you in vain—you had disappeared.

Gret. That is a lie. You never even accused me.

Holmes. It is the truth, I swear it. [*Walks over* L.]

Gret. [*Taking* C.] I don't believe you. You deserted me because you found me a drag and a burden on you when I refused to become an accomplice in your swindling schemes. At first love blinded me to your true character, but when the scales dropped from my eyes and I saw you as you are, I loathed and despised you. Now give me back my child and I will consider it a boon from heaven if I never see your evil face again. Where is she?

Holmes. Far enough from here to be out of your reach. [*Crosses* R.]

Gret. [C.] Tell me where she is or I shall proclaim myself to these friends of yours as the wronged wife of one of the most unscrupulous scoundrels outside of the penitentiary.

Holmes. [*Threateningly up to her.*] You defy me, do you? Whom do you propose to prove yourself?

Gret. Gretchen Stanton, your lawful wife. I have my wedding certificate.

Holmes. You force the truth from me by your threats. You are not and never were my wife.

Gret. Not his wife! This is some trick.

Holmes. [*Taking* C.] My name is Holmes, not Stanton. I married you under an assumed name and the ceremony was not legal. Proclaim yourself, if you choose—they will laugh at you. On the other hand if you will leave this place peaceably and see me tomorrow, I will tell you where to find your child. Raise a disturbance and imperil either my safety or my prospects and you shall never see her again.

Gret. [*Aside.*] Not his wife! Not his wife! Merciful heaven is my reason again deserting me?

Holmes. [*Aside.*] She hesitates—she weakens—the game is mine.

Gret. I accept your terms; but if you are deceiving me, beware! Restore to me my child and for her sake I will not molest you further. [*Crosses* R.] But as surely as you attempt treachery so surely will I tell the police where to find the president of the Colorado Silver Investment Company. There are three indictments hanging over the head of Maurice Stanton for his share in that rascally swindle. Beware! [*Exit* L. I. E.]

Holmes. She has no suspicion of where Leila is, and so long as I can keep them separated, I can compel her silence by threats or coax it by promises. I wonder if that nigger is on the alert? [*Exit* R. U. E. **Leila** *screams off* R. 2 E. *Hurry music to curtain.*]

Leila. Let me go! Let me go!

Find. [*Staggers on* R. 2 E. *with* **Leila** *in his arms, screaming. Puts hand over her mouth.*] Shut up, you little imp!

[**Stella, Carlotta, Col. Derrom, Rosalie and Children** *enter* R. 2 E. **Holmes and Bob** *enter* R. U. E. **Franz,** *still disguised, runs on* L. 2 E. *behind* **Findham,** *lifts the child out of his arms and puts her behind him with* L. *hand drawing gun with* R. *hand. This must be done very quickly, all the action taking place simultaneously. The climax must be very carefully rehearsed.*]

Franz. Stand back! Attempt to hurt so much as vone hair of dot liddle vone's haid und you'll tink de Fourth of Chuly has proken loose. Dot's de kind of a saur-kraut I am.

Curtain.

Bob, Holmes.

Leila.

Findham, Franz.

Derrom.

Rosalie.

Children.

Charlotta.

Stella.

ACT IV.

[*Handsome drawing room in* Col. Derrom's *house. Boxed scene. Center door or archway with portiers. Doors* R. *and* L. *in box. Table with cover on, down* L. C. *chairs. Arm chair down* C. *Carpet down, rugs, chairs, bric-a-brac, etc. At rise* Col. Derrom *with document in hand, enters* R. *door with* Holmes.]

Derrom. You were indeed fortunate in finding this marriage certificate, my dear boy. [*Examines document. Seats himself at table down* L.]

Holmes. [*Sitting in arm chair* R.] Yes. If I had not wanted

to use that old trunk and so turned the contents out on the floor,
I should never have discovered it.

Derrom. Well, armed with this and the certificate of Franz
Von Altenheim's death, nothing on earth can upset your title to
the estate of the late scientist.

Holmes. How about that Quintillion Mining stock? I see by
tonight's paper, that a new lead has been struck and that prospects are very bright. [*Takes newspaper from table and hands
it to* **Derrom** *who puts on glasses and reads.* **Holmes** *stands beside* **Derrom** *and points to article, looking over his shoulder.*]
You see it is by telegraph from their special correspondent at
Butte, Montana. [*Goes L. Aside.*] It cost me a cool hundred
dollars to get that bogus dispatch printed, but if Lemoine and
Derrom bite on the strength of it, it will have proved cheap
enough.

Derrom. Um—ah—[*reads.*]—"One of the richest leads ever
struck in this country has just been found in the Quintillion
Mine. Sales are reported today at 57, which is higher than the
stock has ever stood."

Holmes. [*Leans against* R. *cor. of table.*] Fortune seems to
smile on me just now, for as you know I hold 2,000 shares of the
stock. However, as I shall need some ready money for my trip
abroad, I will let you and **Lemoine** have a thousand at today's
quotation provided you close the deal tonight.

Derrom. [*Rises.*] Well, if this news is correct, that is very
handsome of you.—Let me see. [*Figures on paper.*] That calls
for a check of $57,000. I can't raise so much without Lemoine's
help, but if he is willing to make the deal I'll go into it with him.
Just wait here a few minutes and I'll go over and see him.
[*Goes L.*]

Holmes. [*Follows L.*] Suppose I go with you? He may
need information and a good many points that I have at the tip
of my tongue.

Derrom. That's a good suggestion. Come this way. [*Exit
with* Holmes L. D.]

Franz. [*Pokes his head through portiers, C. and D.*] Peekaboo,
Mr. Holmes—I vas right next to you. [*Throws back portiers and
enters with* Stella.] Now you see what a rascal that feller is?
He don't vant much—he only vants feefty-sefen tausand dollars
for mining stock vich is vorth about feefty-sefen tausand cents.

Stella. But how do you know this, Franz?

Franz. Hush—don't say a vord. Don't you know I vas dot
willian's promised vife? Ha, ha, ha! He has no secrets from his
vife, you know and he tells me all about de racket dis morning.

He's so stuck on me, dot he gifes me tree hundred dollars to buy new dresses and such a tings. How do you like my new suit? A nice tailor-made suit, he tells me, is vat I vant, so I buy me dis.

Stella. How surprised he will be when he finds how implicitly you have obeyed his instruction. [*Sits in arm chair c.*]

Franz. [*Leaning against table.*] Vell, rodder. But choost vait and if I don't start dot chendleman on de road to de penitentiary tonight, his name is Yohann and he's a sauerkraut.

Stella. What did you do with the detective?

Franz. Scared him pooty near to death and den pulled his leg. He will be a vitness against Mr. Holmes vhen ve get pefore a chudge and chury. Vone ting dere is vich I couldn't pick out of eider of dem.

Stella. What is that?

Franz. Vhy for dey vanted to steal dot child. She's a peaudiful shild, aber I don't see vhat Holmes vanted mit her. How could he use her in his business?

Stella. What is his business?

Franz. Schwindlin'.

Stella. [*Rises.*] Rest assured, we will get to the bottom of that; don't you think we are wasting valuable time? Carlotta will be here soon and then— then—oh, well, you understand.

Franz. Yah—I understand [*Puts his arm around her.*] Two was gompany and three's a whole shootin' match—ain't it? Vell! Vell! Vell! Ah! Stella, ven I tink dot you bin de daughter of a rich man it makes me feel frightened dat you have given de sweet flower of your lofe to a poor fellow like me.

Stella. Why dear? What should frighten you? You are poor, it is true, but I shall share your poverty yes and I will work too if you cannot earn enough for both. No matter how poor we may be, no murmur or complaint shall ever pass my lips.

Franz. My noble, beautiful Stella! [*Takes her in his arms.*]

Stella. There is only one thing I ask.

Franz. Name it, and if you ask for the earth I'll find some way to get for you.

Stella. I only ask that you will never love me any less than you do now.

Franz. Dis is mein answer to dot. [*Kisses her.*]

Car. [*Enters c. D.*] Excuse me. [*Turns her back.*] It is all over. [*Turns and comes down.*] I really didn't intend to intrude but what is the meaning of Franz being here? Has the Colonel relented? [**Franz** *places arm chair and* **Carlotta** *sits.* **Franz** *leans against table* L.]

Stella. [R. C.] Not yet. but we've made up our minds to get married and we are going to brave papa's wrath by telling him so tonight, aren't we Franz?

Franz. Yah—you vas goin' to do de tellin' while I back you up. Next ting I introduction of your fodder's shoe maker to mein tailor. Und mein gracious! Vhat heavy boots he has got on tonight. I tell you vot, you chust coax him to put on his slippers before he ses me.

Stella and Car. [*Laugh.*] Ha, ha, ha!

Car. The Colonel and Mr. Holmes are with papa. They are talking business—something about mining stock, outside on the verandah.

Franz. Yah—feefty-seven tausand dollars vorth of schwindle. I know all about dot. Say, dey might come in here—I tink ve better take a valk—come along quick—I tell you someting. [*Ex. with* **Stella** *and* **Carlotta** c. *door.* **Derrom** *and* **Holmes** *enter* L. *door.* **Franz** *listens,* C. D.]

Holmes. That arrangement will be quite satisfactory, Colonel. You sign an agreement tonight to purchase the thousand shares and let me have a check for the amount before the bank closes tomorrow.

Derrom. Certainly, certainly. I'll give you a check for $5,000 on account to bind the bargain. [*Sits at table and writes.*]

Holmes. [*Goes* R.] That is more than satisfactory, Colonel. [*Aside.*] I'll cash that check early in the morning. In case of any trouble from Gretchen, Lena and I can take the first train for New York and this money will be ample for our journey to Berlin.

Derrom. Here is the memorandum. See if it is all right? [**Holmes** *crosses and takes paper.*]

Holmes. [L. C.] There isn't a fault to find. [*Glancing over paper.*]

Derrom. [*Rises and hands check.* **Franz** *enters* C.] And here is the check. That I know is all right! [*As he hands check,* **Holmes** *takes it with same hand as that in which he holds paper.* **Franz** *steps between them and snatches both papers, tears them to pieces and throws them in* **H's** *face.*]

Holmes. [R.] The cobbler. What does this mean?

Franz. [C.] It means dot you vas der biggest confidence man outside de penitentiary. It means that you are trying to swindle dis old chentleman and his friend out of feefty-sefen tausand dollars. It means that you are crooked enough to be der past president for der Ram's Horn club, vich is composed of all der crookedest people on earth.

Holmes. [*Crosses ₁. to* **Derrom.**] The fellow is evidently crazy, Colonel. The best thing we can do is to send for an officer and have him removed.

Franz. Don't get in a perspiration about de officer—you 'll see him pefor you vant him, I pet you.

Holmes. Have I your permission, Colonel, to kick this insulting rascal out of the house?

Derrom. Well, no. [*Crosses* ᴿ.] Not till I hear upon what grounds he makes these charges.

Holmes. What! You surely will not listen to him for a moment! Is it likely that I, heir to the Altenheim property, with the legal proofs of my claim lying on that table, would lend myself to any such wild swindling scheme as this Dutch rascal has charged me with? It is preposterous.

Franz. [*Aside.*] Mein Gott! He said Altenheim! Can it be dot dis is de man I bin hunting for so long? [*Aloud.*] You say you bin de heir to de Altenheim property. I vas Franz Altenheim's best friend yet I never did here him mention your name.

Holmes. I don't believe you ever saw Franz Altenheim. [*Takes paper from table.*] This wedding certificate proves that I was his brother-in-law, married to his sister Gretchen.—[*Hands paper to* **Franz.**]

Franz. [*Looking at document.*] Married! Gretchen married to Holmes, Morris Holmes?

Holmes. You hold the proof of that and again you show that your acquaintance with Franz Altenheim is a mere pretense. Those papers there prove the death of my wife and her child.

Franz. Dead? Mein liddle Gretchen dead? Oh, mein liebe schwester. [*Drops into arm chair overcome with emotion.*]

Holmes. [*Aside.*] His sister! [*Recoils down to* ᴸ. *corner.*]

Gret. [*Enters* ᶜ. *with* **Leila.**] That is a cruel lie! [*Comes down* ᶜ. **Stella** *enters* ᶜ. ᴰ. *with* **Rosalie** *and* **Carlotta.**]

Holmes and Franz. [*Who rises.*] Gretchen!

Gret. [*Holding out arms appealingly.*] Franz, my brother.

Franz. My liddle Gretchen! [*Goes toward her, stops and turns sadly away.*] Aber nicht! You are not mein liddle Gretchen, for dere beside you stands an innocent shild vich is de proof of your shame and disgrace-- Oh, Gretchen, Gretchen! [*Flings himself into arm chair* ᶜ. *covers face with his hands and sobs.*]

Gret. Franz—upon my soul, I say that is not true. [*Kneels and takes his hand.*]

Franz. I vish I could believe dot—but I can't.

Gret. You must, you shall see, on my knees I swear that I am a lawful wife and here is the proof. [*Takes paper from bosom and hands it.*]

Franz. Dere is someting de matter mit mein eyes—I can't hardly see—read me dot, Stella.

Stella. [R. C. *Reads.*] "I hereby certify that on the fourth day of April, 1884, in the city of Antwerp, I did solemnize a marriage, the contracting parties being Maurice Stanton and Gretchen Altenheim. Signed, Gotlieb Neddinger, pastor."

Franz. [*Raises her.*] Gretchen—forgive me—forgive your bruder his, cruel, wicked doubts. [*Embraces her.*] Leila—come and kiss your onkle vich is also your Liber Franz. [*Kisses Leila.*]

Derrom. [L.] So sir, these so-called proofs are forgeries, as this event proves. You shall pay dearly for them. [*Lays hands on* **Holmes.**]

Franz. [C.] Chust hold him a minute, Colonel, till I find out vone ting. Gretchen, vhere is dis man Stanton vich married you?

Gret. [R. C.] There he stands under the name of Holmes.

Holmes. That is my true name. [*Goes* C.] Stanton was merely assumed, the marriage was not legal and your brat there is a—— [*Before he can finish* **Franz** *chokes him, forcing him to his knees.*]

Franz. You most inhuman beast. Vould you try to bring shame upon your own liddle innocent shild?

Rosalie. [R. C. *goes to* **Holmes.**] Oh, you monster. I always knew you were a bad one, but I never thought you were so low down, sneaky and detestable as that. [*Drops down to* R. *corner.* **Holmes** *rises.* **Franz, Gretchen** *and* **Leila** *grouped,* L. C.]

Derrom. [C.] Your law is all wrong, you pitiful scoundrel. The fact that you were rascal enough to marry this poor girl while sailing under false colors, does not make the ceremony illegal. That is the law. [**Holmes** *drops down to* R. *corner.*]

Rosalie. [*Runs to* C. D. *and beckons. Officer enters.*] Do you see that dandy dude down there? [*Up* C. **Derrom** *walks over to* **H.**]

Officer. Yis ma'am.

Rosalie. Are you a friend of mine?

Of. Indade I am.

Rosalie. And you'll do me a favor?

Of. Tin of them, ma'am.

Rosalie. Then take him to the station house and on the way crack his heels against the back of his head till you break his neck.

Of. I will that, ma'am.

Franz. [L. C.] I charge him mit forgery, obtaining money under false pretenses and attempted brigamy. He tried to marry mein schweetheart vhile he vas me a bruder-in-law alretty and his vife vas liffing.

Of. Come on, oura that. [*Handcuffs* Holmes.]

Franz. I vish you had a couple of chains or a clothes line so he couldn't get avay. How vould it do to put him in a barrel and nail on der head?

Of. If he gets away from me I'll give you me month's pay that I dhraw next Choosda. [*To Holmes.*] Come on now, where's his hat?

Ros. I'll get it. [*Gets hat.*]

Holmes. Officer will you oblige me by straightening my hat? [*Officer does so.*] Thanks--awfully—I bid you all good evening—ta, ta. By the way, I have a pair of shoes that need mending and if Mr. Von Altenheim will call tomorrow morning, he may have the job.

Franz. I vouldn't take a good deal to miss seeing you tomorrow morning in de police court.

Holmes. I'm sorry I can't stop with you longer, but my friend's time is somewhat limited and I know you'll excuse me. Ha, ha, ha! Ha, ha, ha! [**Rosalie** *puts his hat on. Exit c. with* **Officer.**]

Ros. [*Mocking* Holmes.] Ha, ha, ha! Now laugh again, will you?

Stella. [L. C.] Now papa, not only did Franz save my life when the horse ran away, but he has preserved our honor by saving me from a bigamous marriage with that wretch.

Derrom. [L. C.] My dear, I fully appreciate Mr. Altenheim at his true value and if sometime in the future, when you are both old enough to know your own minds, you should come to me and ask for a parental blessing, why, I would most probably grant it.

Franz. Tanks. [*Shakes hands.*] Aber I tink ve vas both old enough to know, eh, Stella? [*Takes her around the waist and they whisper, c.*]

Stella. Yes, and we have concluded to get married two weeks from tonight, if your honor please. [*Courtsey.*]

Franz. [R. C.] Oh, vhat's de use of vastin' time? Make it a week from yesterday and be done mit it.

Derrom. My dear Altenheim. [*Crosses* L. *to* Gretchen and Leila.]

Franz. [*Aside.*] Hear dot? Now I vas his dear Altenheim. A few minutes ago I vas only a sauerkraut cobbler. Vell, vell,

vell— vhat a difference money makes —ain't it? [*Aloud.*] My dear Colonel, now dot my schweester and I come into our fortune, I tink better I put de Von before my name, for now mein onkle has gone dead I bin der Baron Von Altenheim.

Derrom. Then all that remains for me to do is to give my consent and say bless you, my children, in the good old fashioned way.

Ros. [*Throws back portiers c. and other* **Children** *enter. Picture.* **Franz** *and* **Stella** *c. with* **Children** R. *and* L. *of them.* **Derrom** and **Gretchen** R. **Rosalie** *up* L. C.]

Franz. Hello liddle vones. Vell, vell, vell, you chust have turned up in time to congratutate your Lieber Franz, vich is now der happiest man in all de vide, vide vorld.

Curtain.

www.ingramcontent.com/pod-product-compliance
Lightning Source LLC
Chambersburg PA
CBHW032141270626
47172CB00009B/815